Sunlight in the Shadows

Sunlight in the Shadows

Gail Newman

Desert Palm Press

Sunlight in the Shadows

by Gail Newman

ISBN (trade): 9781942976578
ISBN (epub): 9781942976585
ISBN (pdf): 9781942976592

Desert Palm Press
1961 Main Street, Suite 220
Watsonville, California 95076
www.desertpalmpress.com

Editor: Glenda Poulter
Cover Design: Michele Bordeur - eebooWORX

Printed in the United States of America
First Edition October 2017

You never know where the road of life might take you.
Just make sure you don't miss the signs.

Chapter One

"HOW THE HELL DID this happen?" Kate slammed her hand on the conference table. She studied the faces of those gathered, looking for an answer.

"Jesus, Kate, don't you think if someone knew they would have said something?" someone seated at the table said.

"I would have hoped so, but apparently that didn't happen, did it? No one knew anything? With all our checks and balances, not one clue. I find it hard to believe but I guess that really doesn't matter at this point. We all know the outcome of this."

***

"How the hell did this happen?" Kate asked herself again weeks later as she sat on the ferry, her overnight case on her lap and her suitcase at her feet. She sighed.

Months earlier, she was a high-powered attorney at Peters and Phips. Now the firm was ruined. Phips embezzled the firm's assets and gambled away the money without anyone noticing. When Federal and local agencies raided the corporate office, anyone with his or her name on an office door had depositions taken and were then sent packing. Like the others, Kate was escorted out of the building.

Emotionally drained, Kate had escaped Manhattan for Bedford, where she knew her parents would baby her. At first, Kate's parents gave her the space she needed and allowed her to wallow in her despair. When Kate first arrived, Morgan explained that she would not push Kate to discuss what had happened unless she wanted to. Her father, David, worked a little harder to let things ride. Kate knew he didn't believe extended wallowing was productive. When he couldn't take it anymore, David had stopped at her room as he left for the office and told her it was time to pick herself up and pull it together. Although Kate attempted to reach out to her contacts, she couldn't muster enough courage to go to the City for an interview.

One morning after David left for work, Kate and her mother lingered at the kitchen table. Kate stared out the window watching the birds play in the birdbath as Morgan poured them each a fresh cup of tea.

"It does so kill me to see you this way, dear-heart." Morgan rubbed Kate's back. "Anything on the horizon?"

Kate shook her head.

"Look, darling, you just have to get back on that horse. Sometimes you have to make things happen. You know, get your knickers in order."

Kate almost spit out her tea. "You know, Mother, you may have left England at an early age, but between the accent that you picked up from Gran and the things you come out with, you really are as British as most real Brits." Kate grabbed her napkin and wiped her lips.

"Well you know, darling, that's one thing about us Brits, stiff upper lip and all that." They both laughed. "Kate, I have something I want to talk to you about. You know I have to head off to London next week and your father will be at a conference, so I was thinking—"

"Oh, Mother! I would love to go to London with you." Kate jumped from her seat and threw her arms around her mother.

Morgan held her. "That was not exactly what I had in mind. I think it would be a good idea for you to head out to Shelter Island and stay with Aunt Connie."

"What?" Kate tried to squirm away.

Morgan held her tighter. "I've called and made all the arrangements."

Kate broke free and covered her face with her hands. "You have to be kidding me. Oh, my god. What did you tell her?"

"Darling, she already knows what happened. I just told her that I was going out of town and you could use a change of scenery to clear your head."

"Oh my god...I'll never hear the end of this. 'How did this happen, Kate? I thought you were doing so well, Kate?' Mother, I can't go there." Kate threw herself into her chair and put her head on the table.

"Katherine Arabella Whitfield, you are going to Aunt Connie's, you are going to decide what you are going to do with your life, and for God's sake, you are going to get hold of yourself."

Kate lifted her head. "Could you get any more dramatic?"

"I thought it was pretty good, if I do say so myself." Morgan patted herself on the back and gave Kate a playful smirk. "Dear-heart, you know how much you love it there. I truly think this will be the best thing for you."

"I loved it there because Gran was there."

"I know, but you know she's there in spirit."

Morgan kissed the top of Kate's head and turned to leave the room. "By the way, you leave on Friday."

Gail Newman

Chapter Two

FRIDAY MORNING, MORGAN DROVE Kate to Penn Station. As she helped Kate pull her bags from the trunk, she gave her a pep talk: "Lighten up, my darling. You know I'm not sending you to some horrible place."

"Great. I'm thirty-five and my mother has to send me someplace."

"Kate, you just need to get your eggs in a basket and your ducks in a row. A good roll in the hay couldn't hurt either." Morgan slapped Kate's bottom.

"Mother!"

"What, darling?" Morgan put on her best innocent face but couldn't keep it up. "Come on...it's not like we haven't been through all of this before. What happened to that adorable assistant you had to fire because you couldn't keep your hands off her?"

"Really, Mom? Really? I'm not depressed enough? You have to go bringing up my love life too?"

"Well, you know what they say, a good orgasm is good for the body and soul."

"That's it, Mother. Kiss me goodbye. I'm sure my train is leaving."

"All right, my girl. I love you. Be sure you call me every five minutes so I know what's going on. When your father gets back from his conference, maybe we will come out for a weekend."

"Sure," Kate said as she picked up her bags, "but I might be back in Bedford by then, so we'd better play it by ear."

A taxi blared its horn. "Hold your horses," Morgan chided back.

"Bye, Mom."

"Bye, sweetheart! Do enjoy yourself...even if it kills you." Morgan hurried off before Kate could reply.

Ugh. Why did Mom have to bring up my love life? It's not like I had a lot of time for a relationship with all the work I did for the firm. Kate frowned before allowing herself a small smile. *Sure had some good one night stands, though.*

At the ferry depot, she bought a one-way ticket. She considered buying a round-trip ticket in case she needed to make a quick getaway, but she decided that if things got bad, she'd swim off the island. That thought made her laugh out loud, despite her mood.

This was the first time she had travelled to the island since her beloved grandmother had passed away. At the ripe old age of ninety-six, Arabella Morgan Hilliard Whitfield left this earth the same way she came in, raising hell. Belle, as she was called by those closest to her, and her sister, Constance, were born into a wealthy family in Cheshire England. Their mother's family was rich, and their father built his fortune raising horses. Arabella and Constance had the best of everything. Both kept low profiles when it came to their wealth, but there was nothing low profile about Arabella's personality. Constantly in trouble for smoking in the bathrooms, missing curfews, drinking, and paying too much attention to the boys, Arabella had a grand time at her parents' expense. It wasn't until she met Kate's grandfather, Edward, that she settled down. After giving birth to their second child, Kate's Uncle Niles, Arabella and Edward moved the family to America.

Shortly after they arrived, Arabella fell in love with a grand mansion overlooking Central Park and it was here that Kate spent her holidays as a child. While visiting friends in the Hamptons, Arabella and Edward snuck away to do a little exploring along the sound. On their way back from Orient Point, on the northern tip of Long Island, they found themselves at the North Ferry in Greenport. They decided to be adventurous and took the ferry to Shelter Island.

Stepping onto the tiny island, nestled between the north and south forks of Long Island, was like stepping back in time, and the moment Arabella arrived, she was hooked. Each time she and Edward visited the Hamptons, they took an excursion to Shelter Island.

On one of their visits, the couple found what they felt was the most perfect place on earth. As they were preparing to leave the island, Edward made a wrong turn, but when he turned down a side street to turn around, Arabella yelled for him to stop the car. Even before the car rolled to a stop, she threw the door open and ran a few feet. Edward joined her and together they realized they'd found their paradise.

"This is it, Edward. This is where we need to be."

Unable to deny Arabella anything, Edward purchased the land, and there they built a house. It was in this house that Constance came to live after Edward passed away, and where Arabella closed her eyes for the last time.

As the ferry bumped into its slip, Kate realized it was already two o'clock, but she wasn't in a hurry. She took her time leaving the ferry. At the edge of the parking lot, she stopped and scanned the cars until she saw her, sitting in her Mercedes convertible—Constance Hilliard in all her glory. Kate couldn't help but think about her grandmother retrieving her from the ferry depot. Kate made her way to her aunt's car.

"Hello, Aunt Connie."

"Why, yes, there you are." Constance got out of the car. "Let me take a look at you, dear."

Kate turned, as she knew her aunt expected, even as she inwardly rolled her eyes. *Don't want to rock the boat right out of the gate.*

"All right, give your auntie a kiss." Kate carefully planted a kiss on Constance's soft cheek. "Let's get your bags in the trunk, shall we?"

Once in the car, Constance adjusted the kerchief that covered her hair. God forbid those 'natural' blond locks go flying about. With that, they were off. Up the hill, past the Victorian homes, past the restaurant where Kate used to have lunch with her grandmother and Constance, and down through town. The entire time Constance making small talk about what was going on at each location. Kate breathed in the salt air as Constance made the left turn toward Dering Harbor. A row of old mansions came into view. Belle's Beauty, Arabella and Edward's dream house, was farther up the road facing the other side of the harbor, in a more secluded area. The long driveway was lined with azaleas that were just coming into bloom. Kate noticed the daffodils in the nearby garden were starting to wane.

Arabella and Constance spent years planting the entire property. Arabella enjoyed gardening on her own, but Kate remembered her grandmother telling her that she most enjoyed it when she could garden with Constance. The two sisters always broke for lunch on the patio overlooking the harbor and sat for cocktail hour in the same location at the end of each day.

When Kate caught sight of the house, she tried to take it all in. Belle's Beauty was built to Arabella and Edward's specifications, and it was an exquisite home. The endless rows of windows lining the all-white structure gave it an old New England feel, but the elaborate trim made it feel like an English manor. Everything looked the same as it did the last time Kate visited, except the shutters and doors were painted a deep blue.

Constance pulled the Mercedes in front of the six-car garage and turned to Kate. "All right, dear, let's get you inside."

After getting her bags from the trunk, Kate followed her aunt up the path toward the house, pausing for a moment to look out over the water.

"Lovely, isn't it, dear?" Constance called from the top of the path.

Kate nodded her head and continued up the path to the side entrance. Kate took a few tentative steps into the mudroom and peered into the kitchen. Kate took a few more steps and stopped again, as if waiting for her grandmother to call out to her. Silence. She walked into the middle of the kitchen now, where Constance was already heating the kettle.

"I'll make some tea. Are you hungry, dear?"

Although Kate hadn't eaten since that morning, she hadn't given much thought to food. "Why, yes, I guess I am."

"Good. Take your bags upstairs to your room, and I'll set out the sandwiches I made before I went to fetch you."

Kate took her bags and headed up the back staircase. It was the staircase the house staff used when the family had employed one. Kate stopped about half way up. She could almost smell the pancakes Mrs. Miller used to make when Kate was a little girl. Kate would bound down the stairs practically tripping over herself to be the first one at the table. It was one of Kate's favorite parts about visiting her grandmother. When Mrs. Miller retired, Constance had taken over the cooking.

Kate resumed her trek up the stairs. When she reached the second floor, she headed down the hallway to her favorite room. She stopped in front of the door to take a deep breath before going in. It was still the same as when she and her grandmother had decorated it. The walls were periwinkle, her favorite shade of blue. White lace curtains hung on the windows over shades drawn to block the sun and protect her privacy, not that anyone could see the house from the road. Arabella always said, "A lady must be allowed her privacy." The blue, white, and pink flowered quilt that her grandmother had sewn still draped the bed. Constance had offered it to Kate after the funeral, but she couldn't bear to take it from its home.

Kate put her bags down and looked around. *God, I miss her.* Just when Kate felt the tears welling up, her cell phone rang.

"Mom?"

"So, are you there yet?"

"Yes."

"Are you okay?"

"No."

"I know, darling. It was hard for me the first time I went back too, but it gets easier every time."

Kate started to cry.

"It's all right, just relax. How's Aunt Connie?"

"She's fine. She looks amazing. How old is she?"

"Well, that depends on who you ask." Morgan chuckled. "Neither one of them ever told their real age, and I only know Mother was ninety-six because I had to approve the headstone. If I had to guess, I'd say she's probably eighty-three or eighty-four."

"No. Were they really that far apart in age?"

"Remember, they lost a brother that was born between them."

"Well, I have to tell you, she sure doesn't look eighty-four...or eighty-three for that matter."

"Darling, I have to go. I'm heading into another meeting. I just wanted to be sure you arrived safely. Call me later, will you?"

"Love you, Mom."

"Love you too."

Kate stood there for another minute debating whether to look in her grandmother's room. Deciding she wasn't ready for that yet, she headed back to the kitchen.

Chapter Three

CONSTANCE HAD A TRAY of sandwiches ready when Kate came downstairs. "It's so pretty out, I thought we might lunch on the patio. Is that all right, dear?"

"We always do, Aunt Connie."

"Well, dear, since things are a little different now, I wasn't sure. Be a dear and carry the pitcher of tea for me, will you?"

Constance led the way to the large brick patio. Kate and Constance settled in their chairs, and Constance poured the tea.

"I tried not to make it too sweet, dear, so if you need more sugar, there's some on the table." With that, Constance passed the plate of sandwiches, and Kate helped herself to half of a tuna sandwich and half of a chicken salad sandwich. The moment she took a bite, memories flooded back. These were the best sandwiches she'd ever had.

"Oh, my god, Aunt Connie, I had forgotten how good these sandwiches were." Kate took another bite. "Is this Gran's recipe?"

"No dear, it's mine." Constance took a bite and smiled.

"I always thought Gran made them." Kate was a little embarrassed she'd given her grandmother credit for the sandwiches all those years and sank a little in her chair.

"Well, dear, your grandmother may have put the tuna and the chicken salad on the bread, but I made the tuna and the chicken salad."

"Oh." Kate sank a little more.

"Are they still good now that you know your grandmother didn't make them?"

"Yes, of course. I didn't mean...yes, they're delicious." *Oh my god, how am I going to survive here?* "Aunt Connie, what did you mean when you said you weren't sure about eating on the patio now that things are different?"

Constance put her sandwich down. "With your grandmother gone,

11

I wasn't sure what customs you might still want to embrace. You came here to spend time with her, not me."

Kate hadn't thought about that. She adored her grandmother. But Kate had sensed that Constance didn't want to have a close relationship with her, so the two just got along.

"Aunt Connie, please, I don't want you to change a thing. I want to do everything like we always do. Believe me, I have had enough change in my life to last a lifetime, and I certainly don't want anything here to be any different."

"All right, dear, now that we've got that settled, more tea?" Kate relaxed. "Goodness, dear, you certainly have been run down the road, haven't you?"

And here she goes, just when I thought it was safe.

"Imagine those people stealing money from their own company and putting all those people out of work. Who will hire you now?"

And there you have it. "Aunt Connie, the employees didn't steal the money. It was one of the partners. Why wouldn't anyone hire me, or anyone else from the company?"

"They might think you were in on it."

"It's been proven that he acted alone."

"Well, then, you should have no trouble at all finding another job. Are you looking?"

Kate was beginning to boil. She thought about throwing the rest of her chicken salad sandwich at Constance but controlled herself. A voice calling from the side of the house saved her from saying something she would have regretted.

"Yoo-hoo, Constance, are you out there?"

"Yes, Patsy, we are." Patsy Bingford was Arabella's oldest friend on the island and quite the comedian. "And who is this precious child you have with you? Come and give old Patsy a hug."

Kate flew from her chair toward Patsy. "Oh Patsy, I'm so glad to see you." Kate hugged her close.

"I bet you are," Patsy whispered.

"Come and sit, Patsy. We have tea and sandwiches out. I'll get you a plate and glass." Constance went inside.

"So, kiddo, how long have you been here?"

"Just about an hour."

"And how long before she started in on you?"

"She just started."

"Good, my timing's still perfect." Patsy grabbed Kate's hand.

Constance returned. "Here we are, Patsy, dear. I'm so happy you stopped by."

"Well, when you told me Kate was coming, I just couldn't wait to see her."

Kate beamed at Patsy. "A visit here would never be the same without seeing you."

Patsy placed a sandwich on her plate. "So, what plans do you have while you are here?"

Constance cleared her throat.

"What? I'm just asking," Patsy said.

"I didn't say anything."

"You didn't have to. You did that 'don't ask,' throat clear thing."

"I most certainly did not, and I have no idea what you are talking about."

"Ah ha." Patsy turned back to Kate. "All right, then, what do you plan to do while you're here?" She shot Constance a victorious look.

Kate looked back and forth between them. "I really haven't had a chance to think about it. Mother sprang this on me just the other day."

"How are Morgan and your wonderful father, I might ask?" Patsy said while still eyeing Constance.

"Both are fine. Mom is leaving for London on Tuesday, and Dad has a conference in Cleveland."

"Give them my best when you talk to them. Hopefully, we'll see them out here soon." Patsy took a quick breath. "So, kid, have you thought about what you are going to do about your career?"

"Patsy, for goodness sake, leave the girl alone."

"Oh, you mean you haven't asked her yet?" Patsy waved her sandwich at Constance.

"Ladies, please." Kate wasn't sure where this was going, but she was sure it was making her uncomfortable. "I guess I'll start looking to see what opportunities are available in the City."

"Or out here." Patsy sipped her tea.

"Out here?"

"Why not? You're a lawyer, aren't you?"

"Why, yes. Yes, I am."

"You don't think people out here ever need a lawyer?"

"I guess so. I hadn't thought about it." Kate was about to take a bite of her sandwich.

"Well, you should. God knows there's money out here as much as in the City. Besides, you're going to need it." Patsy shook her sandwich at Kate.

"Patsy!" Constance chided as she slapped her hand on the table.

Kate decided things were getting strange. "I have savings and the apartment if I need to sell it."

"Oh dear, no. You never sell anything nice in the City once you have it. Otherwise, you will never be able to afford it again."

Constance made a good point but Kate wasn't worried about money. "I'm okay for now, so I'll just concentrate on finding something."

"Sounds good, kiddo," Patsy said. "What are the plans for dinner, Constance? The usual?"

"I think not, Patsy. I mean, Kate just got here, and I don't think—"
Patsy cut her off. "She can come with us."

"It's no big deal if you have plans this evening. I can get settled in," Kate said.

"No. You come with us." Patsy leaned in across the table. "Every Friday night, one of our friends holds a potluck at her house. We all take turns."

"That sounds nice, but why don't the two of you go? I'll be fine. Perhaps I can join you next week. Shall I clear some of the plates?" Kate stood up.

"Thank you, dear. That would be nice."

Kate gathered the plates and headed toward the house. She paused when she heard the two women whispering.

"When are you going to give her the letter?" Patsy asked.

"At the right moment," Constance said.

The letter? What letter? Kate wondered, but not enough to make her stop and ask.

Chapter Four

KATE SAT IN THE window seat, staring out at the gardens below her window. She leaned against the window and sighed. There was so much to contemplate but before she had a chance to commiserate with herself, Aunt Connie spoke from her doorway.

"Are you sure you want me to go, dear? I feel just awful about leaving you alone on your first night."

"Its fine, Aunt Connie. I wouldn't be good company to anyone this evening anyway, whether I went with you or if you stayed home. It will be good for me to get settled."

"All right, dear, if you're sure." A car's horn sounded in the driveway. "That will be Patsy. I should be home before eleven. You have my mobile number if you need me."

"Yes. Don't worry. I'll be fine."

Constance gave Kate a quick nod and was gone. Kate watched as the car disappeared up the driveway and her thoughts returned to the letter she'd overheard her aunt and Patsy mention earlier. *Letter? What letter? Did I even hear that right?* Kate tried to convince herself she was putting too much thought into the whole thing but quickly dismissed that idea. *No, I heard something about a letter. Do I ask her or just wait? I suppose I ought to give Aunt Connie the chance to give it to me on her own, but if she doesn't do it soon, I'll ask Patsy.*

Satisfied with her plan, Kate sighed as she looked around the room. Now what? She wandered around the room familiarizing herself with it again. When she found herself at the doorway, she stepped into the hallway.

Kate made her way to Constance's room and peeked in. The room was decorated in shades of pale lavender and white. On the far side of the room, large windows offered a view of the yard and the harbor. Kate studied the movement of the water for a moment before turning and going further down the hall. She paused at her grandmother's door. *Should I go in? Never mind should I go in, can I go in?* Kate took a deep breath, put her hand on the door knob, and began to turn it. *No. Not yet. I'm not ready.* Shaking her head, Kate went back to her room.

Kate glanced at her alarm clock and saw that it was only seven o'clock and too early to go to bed. *Well, I can read, watch television, or go for a walk.* Deciding on the third option, she grabbed her sweater and made her way downstairs. At the threshold of the living room, she stopped short. *No, I'm not ready to go in there yet either.*

Kate made her way through the kitchen and out the mudroom door. When Kate reached the path to the beach, she stopped to look out over the water. The view never changed, and on a clear evening, she could see the light of the small lighthouse in the middle of the harbor.

As Kate took in the view of the harbor, she thought about how many times she had sailed past the lighthouse in her little sailboat, and about the times her grandmother and Constance would load her in the Boston Whaler and take her for a picnic on a private beach across the harbor. Sometimes, friends would join them and they would picnic all day and have fires on the beach at night. Then there were the family vacations on the large yacht. What a grand time they had. *The boats! I wonder if they're still here and if I can take them out.* It was the most excitement Kate had felt in a while. She would ask Aunt Connie the next day.

In the meantime, what will I do? Kate wandered around the grounds. She spied a bicycle tucked beside the garage and decided she had found her answer. She hopped on and rode down the driveway and out into the street, the wind in her hair and the smell of late spring blooms filling her nose. The sun was low in the sky and the antique streetlights were starting to glow.

Kate headed toward town. As she came around the corner, the lights of the small marina appeared before her. The sunset sky was awash with brilliant orange, gold, and red. The scene was like something from a post card. Kate rode until she met the sidewalk. She chose to push the bike by her side so she could check out the shops. The real estate offices advertised rental opportunities and homes for sale while the merchants featured bathing suits, flip flops, hats, toys, and floats— everything anyone could need for a summer of fun.

As Kate passed the small Seagull restaurant, faint voices drifted into the street. She peered through the open door. Candles burned in little glass holders on the tables and music played in the background. Kate parked the bike alongside the building and went inside.

She was not surprised to see that everything looked exactly as it did the last time she was there. To the left, was a pool table; to the right, a long bar ran the length of the wall, stopping just short of the large front window. A rack of glasses hung over the bar. Small, round tables were scattered between the pool table and the bar. Almost any seat in the house was perfect for watching the activity on the street or the waves in the harbor beyond. In the back was the main dining room that extended onto an outside patio overlooking a picturesque creek.

Kate headed for the end of the bar closest to the front window and took a seat. A few locals at the other end of the bar chatted amongst themselves and didn't acknowledge her. A waitress came out of the kitchen and served the group a plate of appetizers before making her way over to Kate.

"What can I get you?"

"Just a light beer if you have one on tap."

"Sure do." The woman grabbed a glass from the overhead rack and headed for the tap. She returned with Kate's beer and a menu. "Just let me know if you need anything else. I'm Shannon."

"Thanks, Shannon, I will. I'm Kate."

Shannon extended her hand.

"Nice to meet you, Kate."

After they shook hands, Shannon went back to the other end of the bar. Kate turned her attention to her beer. Ice crystals had formed around the lip of the frosty mug just the way Kate liked it. She took a sip and looked out the window at the park that overlooked the harbor and the yacht club. Kate watched an osprey land in its nest on the telephone pole above the street. Kate sighed. For that moment, she felt like she didn't have a care in the world. A voice at the front door caught Kate's attention.

"Did the delivery come?" A woman, whose face was hidden by the boxes of paperwork she carried, came inside. She dropped the stack on the nearest table and headed to the bar.

"What's the matter? Bad day off island?" one of the men at the end of the bar asked.

"Yes, so don't you give me any trouble, you old fool." The woman went around the bar and poured herself a glass of beer and downed it in one gulp. "Ah, that's better."

Shannon came out of the kitchen. "Need help?"

"No. I just need to know if the delivery came."

"Yes."

"Good. Tomorrow should be busy." The woman poured herself another beer and returned to the stack of paperwork she had abandoned. She sat down and immediately went to work.

Kate finished her beer and set the empty glass on the bar. Shannon brought her another.

"Looks like you enjoyed it." Shannon smiled.

"Thanks. I did." Kate raised the glass to her.

Someone from the end of the bar called for Shannon and Kate was alone again. After a few minutes passed, Kate got the feeling she was being watched. She looked to her left at the group at the end of the bar. *Nope, no one down there.* Kate pretended to be looking back at her beer as she stole a quick glance over her left shoulder. *Caught ya!* Kate smirked as the woman at the table buried her head in her paperwork. *Probably curious about who I am and why I'm here alone.* Kate took another sip of her beer. A few more minutes later Kate felt a presence behind her.

"Aren't you Belle's granddaughter, Kate?"

Kate turned and found herself face to face with the paperwork woman.

"Yes, I am."

"Oh, my god, Kate, don't you recognize me?"

Oh my god, no, I don't remember you. She hated when this happened. Her mind raced. *Who is this?*

"It's me, Natalie Brewster. We used to play together all the time when you came out in the summer."

"Natalie?" Memories flooded back to Kate. Swimming. Biking. Sailing.

Natalie was practically jumping up and down in front of Kate as if she were trying to jog Kate's memory.

"Oh my god, Natalie."

Natalie threw herself at Kate. The two hugged and then separated.

"What are you doing here? Didn't you move away?" Kate asked. They hugged again.

"We did, but when my parents got divorced, Mom moved back here to be with her family. After I finished college and worked at a few jobs I hated, I came back and Mom and I bought this place," Natalie said when they finished hugging.

"Get out of here. You guys own The Seagull?"

"I know. Funny, isn't it? You remember we used to ride our bikes up here? If my father was here, we would come in and he'd sit us up on the bar stools and we'd do shots of cola." Natalie giggled.

"That's right. We thought we were so cool." Kate laughed.

"So, what are you doing here?" Natalie sat down on the barstool next to Kate.

Natalie was a little fuller now but she still had that radiant smile and those sparking green eyes. Kate forced herself to focus on the question.

"I came for a little getaway. Kind of figuring out what to do next in my life."

"Aren't we all? I am so sorry about Belle." Natalie patted Kate's hand. "If I hadn't been visiting my Dad at the time, I would have been at the funeral."

"Yeah." Kate finished her beer. "It's weird being here without her."

"I know. I can still see her and Patsy and her other cohorts coming in for lunch or a drink."

"Did they do that?"

"All the time. They still do. Connie comes too."

Kate pictured them all filing into The Seagull and taking siege of the little restaurant. The thought made her smile.

"Let me get you another beer and I'll join you."

Kate put her hand over her glass. "I'd better take it easy. I rode a bike down here."

"Nonsense." Natalie grabbed the glass. "We'll throw the bike in the back of my truck and I'll take you home." Natalie turned to the group at the end of the bar. "Hey, everybody, this is Kate Whitfield, Belle's granddaughter."

A collective "Hello, Kate," came from the end of the bar.

"Hi." Kate waved, smiling ear to ear.

Over the next few hours, Kate and Natalie sat at the bar catching up. Kate shared some about her past, and, once she was comfortable, the fact that she was gay. To Kate's surprise, Natalie didn't seem shocked. Kate also 'fessed up about the law firm debacle. Natalie wasn't surprised about that news either.

"I guess since you saw my Gran and Aunt Connie regularly, you got family updates?" Kate laughed.

"Bits and pieces," Natalie said. Kate got the feeling it was a little more than bits and pieces. "So how are you getting along with Connie?"

"Well, it's just my first day here and..." Kate hesitated.

"She's not Belle," Natalie finished. "I know."

"That's sort of it, I guess. I never paid that much attention to her. I mean, she was there, and that was fine. I just never felt close to her. It was almost like she kind of held back from getting close to me."

"She speaks very highly of you to everyone around here." Natalie motioned to Shannon to bring them another round.

"Really?"

"Oh yeah, it's always, 'Kate's doing this or Kate's doing that.'"

"Wow. I thought she would be talking about my mother or uncle."

"Oh, she talks about them too, but you can see her beaming with pride when she talks about you."

"That really surprises me." Kate raised an eyebrow.

"Maybe there's a whole lot about Connie you don't know."

"Well, I'm going to be here for a while, so maybe I'll find out." Kate glanced at her watch. It was almost ten-thirty. Kate looked out the window. The last time she looked, the sun was setting. Now it was completely dark. "Man, I can't believe what time it is. Sorry to break this up, Nat, but can you take me home?"

"Sure."

As Kate and Natalie finished their beers, Natalie yelled to Shannon to tell her they were leaving.

"Nice to meet you, Shannon. See you again soon," Kate called.

Outside, they loaded Kate's bike in Natalie's truck and made their way to the house.

"So, where are you living?" Kate asked as she pulled the bike out of the truck bed.

"I bought a house just down the creek from the bar. Here's my cell number and the house number. Call me tomorrow and we'll make some plans." Natalie hugged Kate before climbing back in the truck.

"Glad to see you again, Natalie," Kate yelled as she drove off.

Kate put the bike back on the side of the garage and went inside. After grabbing a bottle of water from the refrigerator, a feeling of sadness passed over her. Thinking about it for a moment, she realized that she had never been alone in the house. Instead of allowing herself to wallow in that feeling, she imagined she could hear her grandmother laughing. Smiling to herself, she went up the stairs to her room. Half an hour later, Kate heard a car in the driveway and the sound of a car door slamming. A few minutes later, Constance was standing in Kate's doorway.

"Everything all right, dear?"

Kate looked up from her magazine. "Yes. I took your bike and rode into town to The Seagull. I ran into Natalie Brewster and she brought me home."

"How wonderful. Natalie is such a nice girl. I'm glad she brought you home. You know how dark it is out here at night, with the deer and all."

The deer was a running joke in their family. When Kate and her mother would go for walks, Arabella always made them take a flashlight so they wouldn't get hit by a deer. Kate and her mother always laughed once they were out of earshot because who gets hit by a deer? Then one night, when they were returning from a walk, a herd of deer ran right past them. They never made fun of Arabella's warning again.

"Tomorrow we will take care of your transportation needs. Goodnight, dear. I'll wake you for breakfast." Constance tilted her head and gave Kate a little smile.

"Goodnight, Aunt Connie. See you in the morning." *Take care of my transportation needs? Hmmmm.* Kate wondered what Constance had in mind as she fell asleep.

Chapter Five

THE SUN PEEKED THROUGH the drapes and danced on Kate's face. She woke but remained still for a minute, enjoying the light on her face. After a few minutes, she leaned over to look at the clock. It was eight o'clock. She was surprised as she was usually awake by seven. She started to stretch when she heard a soft tap at the door.

"Are you awake, dear?"

Kate rubbed her eyes. "Yes, Aunt Connie."

"All right. Come down to the kitchen. I'll put the kettle on."

Ah, tea. The one thing Kate had to have in the morning. Kate pulled on a pair of sweat pants and a long-sleeved tee and made her way down the back stairs to the kitchen.

"Good morning, dear." Constance stood by the large stove.

"Morning. Can I help you with anything?"

"No, thank you, dear. Help yourself to some juice. The tea will be ready in a minute. Are pancakes all right?"

"If they're the same pancakes you used to make, that will be fantastic."

Constance pulled the whistling tea kettle off the stove and carried it to the table where she filled two mugs with steaming water. "How lovely that you met up with Natalie last night." Constance was back at the stove pouring pancake batter on the griddle.

"I know. That was so cool. I'm not sure I would have recognized her, so I'm glad she recognized me."

"I think you'll be surprised to find how many people you know are still on the island."

"You think so?" Kate hadn't thought about that.

"Why yes, dear. Many people who left came back and many people never left at all."

Constance brought two plates of pancakes to the table and sat down.

Kate felt like she was ten years old again. "Oh my god, these are good."

"Glad you like them, dear."

Kate and Constance made small talk as they ate. Kate was careful to remember Constance's rule of no talking with your mouth full. When she was little and visited her grandmother, she always had so much to tell her she couldn't contain herself and often tried to talk and chew at the same time.

"Let her speak, Connie," Belle would say.

"She needs to learn her manners," Constance would respond. Every time. Always the same thing.

When Kate and Constance finished their pancakes and tea, they cleaned off the table and put the dishes in the dishwasher.

"I'll finish up, dear. Why don't you go freshen up and get dressed? We have some things to take care of."

"Okay."

Things to take care of? Kate assumed Constance was referring to her transportation needs, as she called it. Kate took a quick shower and then stood in front of the mirror. For a moment, she saw her ten-year-old reflection looking back at her. Kate took a step back from the mirror and studied herself. Slightly older, of course, but still pretty much the same, she decided. Same long dark brown hair, only with a better haircut so it was less wild than back then. Same deep blue eyes, same build, although she had filled out in all the areas that counted. At five-foot-eight, she was tall enough to model and had, at one time, considered it. But once she became interested in law, she was less concerned with the prospect of modeling. Kate finished drying off and pulled on a pair of jeans, slipped a lightweight, pale yellow sweater over her head and went downstairs.

Constance was still in the kitchen. She turned when Kate entered. "You look nice, dear. Now let's take a walk, shall we?" Kate followed Constance out of the house and down the pathway to the garage. "We need to talk about how you are going to get around while you are here."

Ah, so I was right. This is about my transportation needs.

Constance walked to one of the garage doors and keyed a code on the keypad. The door opened slowly but smoothly. When it was halfway open, Kate could see inside. She gasped. Arabella's 1976 Mercedes 450SL, she bought as a gift for herself when Kate was born, sat inside. Arabella always told people she got two gifts that year—Kate and the car, but that Kate, of course, was the better of the two. The car was a creamy yellow—Mercedes called it butternut yellow—with a dark, camel colored interior and convertible top.

Constance touched Kate's arm. "This is yours now, dear."

"What? Oh my god." Kate tried to absorb what Constance just told her. Kate started to cry.

"Oh no, now don't cry dear." Constance patted Kate's back. "It was always your grandmother's intention that you have this car."

Kate cried harder. "I can't believe it." She touched the car's hood. "I don't think I can." She found it hard to breathe.

"Now, dear, I think you know how your grandmother felt about this car. She never drove it in the rain, always kept it parked in the garage, and had it washed, waxed, and serviced regularly. She always had a little runabout car to use in inclement weather or when she had heavy errands to run, so you are going to need another car for the same reasons."

Constance walked to the next garage door. Again, she keyed in a code and Kate's hand flew to her mouth. A brand new black Range Rover Sport sat inside the garage.

"Uh, Aunt Connie, this is a Range Rover."

"Yes, dear. I called the nice salesman at the dealership and asked him to bring something safe for you to get around in."

"You rented this from the dealership?" Kate couldn't believe it.

"No, dear. Why on earth would I do that? I bought it for you."

"You *bought* this for me?"

"Yes, dear, is there something wrong with it? It looks quite lovely to me."

"Oh, Aunt Connie." Kate started to cry again. Before she could think about what she was doing, she hugged Constance. Her aunt seemed caught off guard and, at first, Kate thought she was going to step back, but instead, Aunt Constance returned Kate's hug. Kate composed herself and the women broke apart.

"Now, dear, we do have to get all the paperwork in order, but I did make arrangements so that you would be able to temporarily drive the vehicles until you can get to the Department of Motor Vehicles. In the meantime, would you like to take a drive off island? I'd like to go to some farm stands." Constance straightened her blouse.

"All right." Kate was still a little in shock.

"Would you like me to drive, dear, or would you like to take one of these?"

Kate thought for a moment. "Why don't we take the Range Rover?" Kate knew the first drive she took in her grandmother's car would have to be taken alone and not until she was ready.

"Fine. Let's go back to the house and I'll get everything we need. Don't forget your license."

Kate followed Constance back to the house but stopped for a moment at the top of the path and looked back at the garage. She still couldn't believe her eyes. After they collected everything they needed, the two headed back to the garage. Constance told Kate the passcodes for garage doors. Kate punched in the code for the Mercedes first. As the door closed, Kate bent down so she could glimpse the car for a second longer before it disappeared.

Kate got in the Range Rover and started it. She was impressed. She had done well for herself, but the Range Rover was fancier than what she was used to. Kate pulled the vehicle out of the garage so Constance could get in.

"This is very nice," Constance said as she inspected the interior of the Range Rover.

"Aunt Connie! Didn't you even look at it when it came?" Kate started down the driveway.

"Why yes, I looked, but I didn't get in. They told me it was, what did he say? Top of the line, and of course that's always what one wants when buying something important."

"Well, you couldn't have done any better. Thank you so much, Aunt Connie. You have no idea what this means to me." Kate touched Connie's hand.

"You are most welcome, dear."

When Kate and Constance pulled into the ferry line, they were delighted to see the ferry had just arrived and was already unloading cars and passengers. They wouldn't have to wait long. While they waited, Kate took the opportunity to check out the controls in the Range Rover. Constance pulled the owner's manual from the glove box and thumbed through it. Once on the ferry, they continued to examine the controls. By the time the ferry pulled into the mainland terminal, Kate was excited to get on the road so she could check out what the SUV could do.

They headed to the North Fork farm stands so Constance could stock up on fresh vegetables, cut flowers, and breads. Kate was surprised when Constance suggested they take advantage of a wine tasting at one of the vineyards. She was even more surprised at

Constance's knowledge about the wines they tasted. They selected several wines they favored and headed back to the island. Kate looked out over the water as the ferry made its eight-minute crossing of the bay.

Constance looked at her watch and turned to Kate. "Are you hungry, dear?"

Kate hadn't thought of the time since that morning. They had been gone for several hours. "What did you have in mind, Aunt Connie?"

"Why don't we take a bottle of wine and stop at the Rose and Thistle for lunch?"

Kate hesitated for a moment. The Rose and Thistle had been her favorite place to go with her grandmother. Even though Constance had joined them on occasion, it was their special place. "That sounds fine, Aunt Connie."

Constance smiled and sat back in her seat. At the restaurant, Kate parked away from the other vehicles in the lot and inspected the Range Rover thoroughly before she could walk away. As she made her way up the steps to the restaurant, she couldn't help looking back at it.

It was a glorious day and Constance suggested they sit outside. She selected a table next to the pink and blue hydrangeas that were just coming into bloom. From the table, they had a perfect view of the small cove across the street. The server arrived with a corkscrew and opened their bottle of wine. Once it was poured, Constance offered a small toast.

"It's very lovely to have you here, dear, and I hope that you will be able to find your way to what will make you happy."

"Thank you, Aunt Connie. This is the one place on earth that brings me pure joy." Kate choked back the tears as she finished speaking.

Before the sound of Kate's voice faded, they heard her. "Yoo-hoo! I thought that was you. See, I told you." Patsy, followed by three other women, headed their way.

"Oh, my," Constance said under her breath.

"Why, Connie, we were just talking about you," the short woman behind Patsy said. "Patsy was just telling us that your niece was in town and here you are."

By now the ladies were dragging chairs over to the table and joining them. "Scoot over, Connie. All right I'll do the introductions," Patsy announced. "Ladies, this is Kate, Belle's granddaughter and Connie's grandniece."

"Hello Kate," the other ladies said in unison.

Patsy looked directly at Kate. "Kate, this is Ms. Lawrence. She is our local artist." Patsy gestured at the short woman who spoke when they approached.

"This is Ms. Kessler. She is our opera aficionado." Slightly taller than Ms. Lawrence, Ms. Kessler had dark hair and big brown eyes.

"Last but not least, we have Doctor Bellows, our resident medic." Ms. Bellows had beautiful blonde hair and bright green eyes. She greeted Kate with a warm smile that made Kate like her immediately. Kate stood up and shook each of their hands.

"It's a pleasure to meet you, ladies."

The barrage of questions started immediately. Patsy whistled. "Ladies, please! One at a time. Let's not scare the poor girl. And first and foremost, where is that waiter with our wine?" Patsy looked around.

As if on cue, the waiter approached the table followed by a bus boy with bottles of wine and glasses. They raised a toast to welcome Kate, then the serious grilling began. They asked her about her childhood, her teenage years, and her college years. Ordinarily, this kind of interrogation would have irritated the shit out of Kate, but she realized these women were her grandmother's dearest friends, and somehow that made it okay, at least until the questions about her love life started.

"So, my dear, have you a significant other?" asked Doctor Bellows.

Constance squirmed in her seat. *Interestingly put*, Kate thought as she poured some wine for herself and Constance. "Actually, no. Not at the moment."

"Perhaps you'll find love on the island," Ms. Kessler said.

"What would you be looking for in a person?" Ms. Lawrence went in for the kill.

Kate thought about that for a moment. "Well, she would have to be someone strong in her convictions, yet sensitive and caring, and she would have to love to have fun." *There. I just outed myself to the whole ladies' club.* Despite the background noise of the restaurant, Kate swore she could hear a pin drop. The ladies looked at one another.

Patsy broke the silence. "Now really, Kate, she shouldn't be *that* hard to find. We'll help you."

Everyone collapsed into laughter.

"Whew." Kate wiped her brow. "Good to know I won't have to go it alone. And with you guys looking out for me, I'm sure I'll be slapping them away like flies."

The women erupted in laughter again. When they finally settled down, the volley began.

"What about Helen's daughter? She might be nice."

"No. I think she just got married."

"Didn't she marry a woman?"

"No. That was Ann's granddaughter."

"So, who am I thinking of?"

Kate and Constance sat back and observed the show.

"I know!" Patsy slammed her hand on the table. "You'll come with us to Friday's potluck. We'll start the hunt there."

Kate couldn't believe her ears. "Um, ladies?" But Kate was too late. The women were busy planning. Kate looked at Constance, shrugged her shoulders, and poured them both more wine.

Eventually, Kate and Constance were able to pull themselves away from the group and head home. They sat in comfortable silence on the ride home, but as soon as Kate pulled in the driveway, Constance burst into laughter. Kate thought she was crying at first because all she could see was Constance's shoulders shaking. Once she realized Constance was laughing, Kate couldn't help but laugh as well. They laughed until they were almost in the house.

"Can I get you anything, dear?" Constance said as she stood staring in the refrigerator, but before Kate could answer, Constance turned around with a bottle of wine in one hand and cheese in the other. "I thought we might sit on the patio and watch the sunset."

"Sounds good to me."

"There are some crackers in the pantry, dear. Bring those, would you?" Constance headed out with the tray. They settled on the patio and looked out over the harbor.

"I could stay here forever," Kate sighed.

"I'm glad you feel that way, dear," Constance said.

Chapter Six

THE RINGING OF KATE'S cell phone woke her from her blissful sleep. "Mmmm. Hello?"

"Good morning, dear-heart. How is my girl this morning?"

"Mom?"

"Someone's still sleepy," Morgan said in a sing-song way.

"Well, that might be because it's eight o'clock on Sunday morning."

"I'm sorry, dear, but with me leaving on Tuesday and your father leaving tomorrow, we were both up early this morning and I wanted to find out what was going on out there. You realize I haven't heard from you since Friday?"

"You are not going to believe it, Mom." Kate sat up.

"Is everything all right?"

"Yes. It's not a bad unbelievable, it's just *been* unbelievable."

"Do tell. Wait. Hold on. Your father wants to hear too. I'm putting you on speaker."

"Hi, honey," David said.

"Hi, Dad. I miss you."

"I miss you too."

"David, darling, call her later if you want to chit chat. I want to hear what's going on."

"I rode Aunt Connie's bike into town on Friday night while she and Patsy were at a potluck and I ran into Natalie Brewster. She and her mom own The Seagull and we caught up on old times." Kate adjusted the pillow behind her.

"How is Patsy? How I do love that woman," Morgan asked.

"Crazy as always. She is just the best. Anyway, I hung out with Natalie and had a great time."

"You didn't ride the bike home in the dark, did you?"

"No. Natalie drove me and then when Aunt Connie got home, she told me we'd take care of my transportation needs in the morning."

"Well that sounds exciting. What happened?"

"Mom, stop interrupting and let me finish." Kate waved her hand in the air.

"Honey," Kate's father chimed in. "You know your mother can't be quiet too long. Ouch. She just hit me."

"So, Saturday morning she makes breakfast—"

"What did you have?"

"Dad!"

"What? She makes a good breakfast."

"Pancakes, okay?"

"Yum. Why don't we have pancakes more often, Morgan?"

"Can I finish my story, Dad? After breakfast, Aunt Connie took me out to the garage. She opened one of the doors to show me Gran's Mercedes. Then she tells me Gran left it to me."

Silence.

"Hello? Did anyone hear me?"

"Dearest, that's really wonderful. We are so happy for you," Morgan said with no surprise in her voice.

"That's it? No oh, my god, or anything?"

"To be honest, honey, we already knew that your grandmother intended to leave you the car," David said.

"What?" Kate took the phone away from her ear and stared at it for a second. "What do you mean you already knew?"

"Mother told me years ago that she planned to give you the car," Morgan said.

"Wow. I can't believe you kept that from me."

"We didn't keep it from you. Your grandmother had planned to give it to you, but given the circumstances, she didn't get a chance."

"But what about Aunt Connie?"

"Your Aunt Connie knew your grandmother's intentions, so we all agreed that when the time was right, she would tell you about the car."

Kate was silent for a moment. Her grandmother's death had come as a surprise, but she had been in her nineties.

"Okay, well get this, after I recovered from finding out the car is now mine, Aunt Connie starts going on about how Gran never drove it in the rain or snow and how she had another car for errands, and then she opens another garage door and there is a brand new black Range Rover Sport that she bought for me."

"Oh, my god. What did you just say?" Kate heard her mother click off the speaker phone.

"She bought me a Range Rover."

"Are you sure, dear, that she didn't she just borrow it or something?"

"Nope. That's what I asked. She said she had a man from the dealership bring something over that would be safe for me. Yesterday morning she gave me all the paperwork I need to drive them until I can get to DMV. We took a ride to the North Fork to some farm stands and wineries and I drove the Range Rover. It's unbelievably cool."

"Will wonders never cease?"

"On our way back, she suggested we have lunch at the Rose and Thistle. I was a little reluctant at first because of Gran, but I figured what the hell, and so we went and had a great time."

"Sounds lovely."

"No sooner had we sat down than along comes Patsy with three of her posse who proceed to grill me about my love life, and then determined they need to make it their project to help me hunt for love."

"What does that mean?"

"Apparently they're going to help me find a girl." Kate held her breath while she waited for her mother to take it all in. Her mom started laughing. "I knew you would like that."

"Sorry, darling, but that's quite a thought. Patsy and friends helping you find a girl."

"Hey, who knows? Maybe they have someone good in mind. It'll be fun to see who they come up with."

"Who were these ladies?"

Kate told her their names.

"I know exactly who these ladies are. Mother was friends with them for years."

"Really? I don't remember them."

"Well, Mother always had various people around, but Patsy's always been a permanent fixture."

"Doesn't matter, I had a good time with them. Aunt Connie and I came home and sat on the patio and watched the sun go down and the stars come out. It was really a nice day."

"I'm so glad, dear-heart. Go and enjoy today, and I'll speak to you later. What? Excuse me, dear. Your father is saying something. What are you saying, David? Yes. Okay. Dear-heart, I will fill your father in on the rest of the conversation, and he will call you from Cleveland. Love you, darling."

"Love you too, Mom."

Chapter Seven

KATE SPENT THE NEXT few days reacquainting herself with the house and grounds. She helped Constance tend the flower beds and get them ready for their summer glory. She cleaned out the boathouse and made sure the small sail boat and skiff were in good shape. The larger boat was dry docked at the local marina. Kate called Natalie to see if they could get together, but Natalie was busy stocking the bar and restaurant for the season. They made plans for Kate to go to The Seagull on Saturday night.

When Kate woke up Friday morning, she found Constance and Patsy on the patio. The two were laughing hysterically over something. Kate smiled as she grabbed a few glasses and headed outside to share the orange juice she retrieved from the refrigerator. Constance and Patsy had already been working on coffee and croissants.

"Good morning, dear." Connie gave Kate a wave and a soft smile.

"Morning, kiddo." Patsy had been laughing so hard she was wiping tears from her eyes.

"You two look like you're having fun." Kate placed the glasses on the table and poured them each some juice.

"Hope you have something to kick that up a notch." Patsy glanced at Constance and then Kate. She was serious. Apparently, the coffee they'd been drinking wasn't doing the trick.

"Patsy, really," Constance scolded.

"What? You know you want something too. You don't have to be so prim and proper just because Kate's here. Kiddo, go back in the house and get a bottle of bubbly from the fridge, would you?" Patsy shooed Kate off.

Kate went inside, took a bottle of champagne from the refrigerator, and looked out the window. Constance appeared to be scolding Patsy, but Patsy wasn't having it and just waved her off. Finally, Constance grabbed Patsy's hand and held it as if the two were in a standoff. A moment later the two women were laughing hysterically again.

Kate wondered what was so funny but decided she wouldn't ask. When Kate returned to the table with the champagne, she opened it and topped off each glass.

"So, what's your plan for the day, dear?" Constance asked.

After they clicked their glasses together, Kate said, "I'm going to drive into Southampton. Someone I knew in law school works in a firm there. I thought I would check it out."

"Interesting." Patsy sipped her drink. "Looking to get some ideas to start your own firm?"

"My own firm? Well, I hadn't really thought about going that far."

"Why not? If you're going to do something, you might as well go big."

"I just want to see what options are out here and go from there."

"Are you joining us for potluck tonight?" Patsy sipped her mimosa.

"Yes, Patsy. I'll be joining you tonight."

"That's wonderful, dear." Constance picked up her glass and smiled at Kate.

"Just be ready at six. I'll pick you up."

"Why don't I drive, Patsy?" Kate asked.

"Fine," Patsy said. "You can pick me up and I'll navigate. Connie and I will take care of the food. You bring the wine."

"Sounds good to me." Kate thought she made out well in the arrangement.

"And, kiddo, you might want to get four bottles."

"No problem. Any particular kind?"

"Nope, we'll drink anything." Patsy laughed.

Constance, looked a little disapproving, sipped her drink but said nothing.

***

Two years had passed since Kate had visited the Hamptons. She drove with the windows open so she could take in the smells of the area and get a better view of the shop windows. When she neared the law office, she found a parking space within a short walking distance.

The Brooks, Brodman, Brodman, and Matthews law firm was in a building mid-block. Kate smiled at the receptionist as she entered the lobby. After telling her she was there to see Dexter Brodman, Kate thought back to when she first met Dex.

One day, during a boring first year business law class, a balled-up piece of paper landed on her desk. The note read...'If you are as bored as I am, escape with me for a cup of coffee. Get up and walk out of the lecture hall. No one will notice. By the way, I'm the handsome guy two rows behind you on the left.'

Kate chuckled and played along. When she glanced over her left shoulder, she was met with a big smile and a small wave. *Okay, I'm desperate enough to get out of here that I'll have coffee with a cute guy.* She picked up her books and the next thing Kate knew, his arm was looped through hers and she and the cute guy were heading out the door together.

"Hi. I'm Dexter Brodman. Dex for short," he said when they were outside. He held out his hand.

Kate shook his hand. "Hello. I'm Katherine Whitfield. Kate for short."

"Well, how interesting that we are both short for something." They laughed. "Shall we go to the Campus Bean?"

"But of course."

Over coffee and the next few hours, Kate and Dex became fast friends. They had many things in common, including their love of law, sports, and drinking. The more they talked, the more they shared and found how alike they were. Until it came to one important aspect of Kate's life.

"Gay? Are you sure?" Dex held his head.

"Yes. It's the one thing in my life I am absolutely sure of."

"Wow. What are the chances I find the girl of my dreams and she's gay?"

From that day they were best friends, but Dex never got over the fact that Kate was gay. He called her his 'Kate of hearts,' and with each of his failed college relationships, and every time he had too much to drink, he told her he was in love with her and couldn't stand that he couldn't have her. It almost ended their friendship, especially the day he finally lost it.

"Just stop this nonsense, Kate."

"What are you talking about?"

"Be with me. You know I love you. I'll take care of you and provide for you, and you, well you'll learn that this is the way it should be."

"The way it should be? Do you hear yourself? What's next? Are you going to force yourself on me so I'll get used to that too?"

They didn't speak for two weeks until one night when the sound of something hitting her window woke Kate. When she looked out the window, she saw Dex on the grassy lawn below, holding a sign that said, 'I'm an idiot.'

She opened the window. "You got that right."

Nonetheless, she threw on some clothes and went downstairs. He promised never to do that to her again. He missed his friend and wanted her back. Kate admitted that she missed him too, but promised to drop-kick him into the next year if he ever said anything like that to her again. They hugged and made up.

Right after they graduated, Dex met Judy. On his wedding day, Dex confided to Kate that there would never be anyone who could replace her in his heart, but that he was happy and loved Judy. Over the years, Kate and Dex remained close, but kids and work inevitably got in the way. As soon as Kate knew she'd be on the island, she had called Dex and was glad to have this chance to reconnect.

Kate looked up as a handsome, dark haired man came into the lobby from the inner offices.

"There's my Kate of hearts." Dex swept her into a hug.

"Dex, oh my god, it's so good to see you." Kate returned his hug.

Dex held her at arm's length. "God, you look beautiful. Too bad my father isn't here today. He would have enjoyed finally meeting you."

"You're in practice with your Dad? I wondered who the other Brodman was. I hope he's doing well."

"We've been working together for the last five years, and he's doing quite well. Come on back to my office." They walked to the offices arm in arm.

"So, what do you think? Not bad for such a lazy clown, huh?" Dex asked as he opened the door to his office.

The office had floor-to-ceiling mahogany shelves, deep rich fabric on the chairs and sofa, and a huge old, refinished desk.

"Not bad at all! Looks like someone does pretty well, actually."

Kate wandered around the office taking it all in but stopped when she got to the pictures that lined the credenza. Front and center was a black and white photo from their graduation day. The two of them smiled brightly into the futures that lay ahead of them. Kate, Dex, and their friends had so much to look forward to. A picture of a woman and two small blonde children drew her attention away from the graduation picture. She picked it up and turned to Dex.

"How are Judy and the kids?"

"Great. Everybody's great." Dex took the picture from Kate and stared at it for a minute. "Grayson is starting middle school this year, and Madison, well, she is still deciding whether or not she wants to go into second grade. She had so much fun in first. She thinks she wants to go back." Dex laughed.

"And Judy?"

"Judy is fine. She's still working as an administrator at the hospital and doing her volunteer work."

"I'm glad you're happy, Dex."

"And what about you, Kate? You getting there?"

Kate sat in one of the chairs facing Dex's desk. Dex turned the other chair to face her and sat down.

"Well, it sucked for a while there. It really did. But I'm feeling better being out here and reconnecting with you." Kate reached out and took Dex's hand.

"Hey, that reminds me. A while ago I came across this file and the name on it sounded familiar. I didn't think too much about it until you called and said you were coming out. That's when it hit me. It's your aunt, Constance Hilliard. My father handles all her stuff and, apparently, your grandmother's as well."

"Get out of here!" Kate pushed on his knee.

"Really. My father has been their attorney for over forty years."

"Oh my god. What are the chances of that?" Kate shook her head. "So, lawyer to lawyer, what do you know?"

"I know that my father took the file and wouldn't tell me a thing when I told him who you were." Dex took a breath and shifted gears. "I'm so glad we're reconnecting. Since you wouldn't marry me, I'm thinking this is the best I'm going to get."

"Dex, stop it. You're terrible. I told you from the moment we met that I was gay and no matter how many times you tried to get me to sleep with you, nothing was going to change that. So 'best non-sexual friend' was all I had to offer."

"I know. Someday my heart will get over it." Dex patted his chest with his hand.

"Yes, someday, but in the meantime, I need your help." Kate got up and began to walk in circles around his chair. "When I first arrived on the island, my grandmother's friend said something interesting that got me thinking. She said if I could be a lawyer anywhere, why not here?"

"Okay. So, what are you thinking?"

"That's where I need your help. What type of lawyer is needed out here?"

"Well, divorce or real estate immediately comes to mind." Dex tapped his chin with his finger

"Too boring."

"Criminal? It gets interesting out here."

"No. I could never defend someone I knew was guilty."

"What about inheritance or estate planning? There are so many older people who don't know how to manage their money or what to do with it if they have a lot of it."

"Now that could be interesting. I bet there are a lot of people out here who get involved in scams or don't understand bills and end up getting sued for something that never should have gone that far." Kate paced the length of the office. "I could start off talking to some of the locals or my aunt's friends and see what's going on."

"Sounds like you at least have a direction." Dex watched her pace.

"I'm going to a potluck with her tonight. Maybe I can get some information then. That should be enough to give me some ideas." Kate sat back down. "See, just seeing you was a source of inspiration."

"I'm glad to know I'm still good for something." Dex smiled. "There's always something going on at this time of year. It'll be easier to get your name out there. Look, now that you're out here, you have to come for dinner."

"Sounds like a good idea to me. And, you'll have to come to the island, of course."

"Maybe I'll surprise you one day and take the drive with my father when he comes over."

"How often does he come to see my aunt?"

"Once a month, I think."

"Well, we'll definitely be seeing each other soon then."

Dex walked her out to the street and hugged her again.

"It's been good to see you, Kate."

Something, I don't know what, but something is going to come out of all this. She thought as she drove back to the island with a smile on her face and a new sense of wellbeing permeating her soul.

Chapter Eight

THAT EVENING, KATE AND Constance arrived at Patsy's house promptly at 5:45. "I'm sure Patsy will be out in a few minutes. She does tend to run a little late no matter how many times I tell her what time I will pick her up," Constance said adjusting her seatbelt. "We will stop by one afternoon so she can give you the tour of the house."

"I'd love to see the house again," Kate said as she strained to see as much of it as she could. Another grand house she couldn't wait to get back inside.

Down the street from Constance's house, Patsy's house also overlooked the harbor. The long, tree-lined driveway led to an old farmhouse that Patsy maintained meticulously.

"I've forgotten, how long has she lived here, Aunt Connie?"

"Well, dear, she and her husband moved to the island after he sold off his chain of clothing stores and Patsy retired. I would guess that would be forty years now."

"Wow. Wasn't she a model at one time?"

"That's right, dear. Then she became a buyer for some of the top department stores."

"How did she meet Gran?" Kate was still looking around at the grounds.

"They met at some charity event in the city."

"Has she always had that killer sense of humor?"

Constance chuckled. "One would have hoped it would have eased with age, but not with Patsy."

"I'm sure once you started living out here, the three of you were quite a force to be reckoned with."

"We may be down one with the loss of your grandmother, but we still are, dear, we still are."

The front door opened and Patsy appeared. "There you are, Patsy.

Do you need help?" Constance called out the car window.

Patsy opened the back door and slid a bag onto the back seat next to Constance's dish and then slid in beside it "Maybe on the way back after I've had a few, but I'm good to go now."

Kate couldn't help but giggle. Patsy gave some quick directions, and they were off.

"What did you make, Patsy dear? It smells wonderful."

"It's my famous crab cakes and coleslaw. And what did you make?"

"I did my version of Lobster Newburg."

"Wow, ladies. I'm impressed. You go all out for these potlucks." Kate inhaled the aromas.

"That's right, kiddo. If there's one thing we like better than drinking, it's eating good food. So, how was your day in Southampton?"

"It was great. I went to see my old friend, who, by the way, is related to someone you know, Aunt Connie."

"Who might that be, dear?"

"I went to see Dexter Brodman, who as it turns out, is the son of yours and Gran's attorney."

"Richard Brodman's son?"

"Yes."

"My, what a small world." Constance turned to look back at Patsy.

"Gets smaller all the time," Patsy said.

"Yes, and Dex only found out recently that his father knew and worked for you both all these years."

"How interesting," Constance said.

"Isn't it?" Patsy tapped Kate on the shoulder and pointed to Kate to turn left.

"Why, that's lovely dear. You will have to meet Richard next time he comes around."

"I never met him when I was in college, so I'd sure love to." Kate pulled the Range Rover down a long driveway and parked behind several other cars that were already there. It was a lovely little house, lit with landscape lighting and lanterns. They gathered their bags, with Patsy making sure Kate did not forget the wine.

As they entered the front door and made their way into the large living room, they heard laughter coming from the kitchen.

"All right, girls, let's get this party started," Patsy yelled as she entered the kitchen. Constance was behind her and Kate filed in last. Kate recognized the three ladies from the afternoon at the Rose and Thistle but she did not recognize the other five. But as soon as Patsy put her bag down, she made the introductions.

Patsy opened one of the warming ovens and slid her crab cakes and Constance's Lobster Newburg onto the rack. She added the coleslaw to the dishes that were already on the kitchen table. With the food prepped, Patsy turned her attention to the wine.

"Nice choice, kiddo," she said after she took a sip.

Constance had already moved on and was involved in another conversation.

"Is this the normal crowd?" Kate asked.

Patsy did a quick turnaround. "Pretty much, give or take a few. It all depends on who's away or has family in. So, tell me about you and Dex."

"What about me and Dex?"

"Come on, you are obviously the Kate that broke the poor boy's heart."

Kate's own heart skipped a beat. "You know about—"

"Look, kiddo, Richard Brodman's been my attorney all these years too, so it's hard not to get to know the person who's handling your affairs. We just never put two and two together that you were *the* Kate."

"So, what was said?" Kate took a long drink of her wine.

"Nothing to get your panties in an uproar about. Just that his son had been in love with some girl in school and, for whatever reason," Patsy winked twice, "the girl didn't have the same feelings. Of course, now we know why." Patsy chuckled and bumped Kate with her shoulder. "Next thing we knew, he was getting married and having kids. She's a nice girl, his wife."

"Yes. I've met her."

"Well, I'm sure you'll be seeing a lot more of them now that you're here."

"Does Aunt Connie know that story?"

"Of course. So, did he give you any ideas about work?"

"We talked about the usual. Divorce."

"No."

"Real estate."

"No."

"Criminal."

"No."

"Then he mentioned inheritance and estate planning." Kate took a sip of her wine.

"Now that sounds good." Patsy popped a shrimp in her mouth. "I can't tell you the number of my friends who have financial troubles because some numb nut screwed up their medical billing, or have trouble collecting an inheritance when all the long-lost relatives came out of the woodwork to contest the will. Now *that* really pisses me off." Patsy popped another shrimp in her mouth. "Damn, if I didn't talk to you or give it to you while I was alive, I certainly don't want you to have it when I'm dead."

Kate smiled. "Well, yes. I was thinking something along those lines. I just haven't figured it out yet."

"I'm sure you will." Patsy gave her a quick hug. "Come now. Let's see what's going on with these old ladies."

Conversation was going fast and furious in the living room, but the conversation slowed when Kate and Patsy joined the group.

"What?" Patsy looked at them. "If you have something you want to talk to the girl about, go ahead. She's not afraid of you."

"Don't be silly, Patsy. We're just talking amongst ourselves." Ms. Lawrence smiled.

"Oh, please. How long have I known you? I certainly know when you're up to something." Patsy waved her finger at them.

Constance stepped forward. "Patsy, dear, I can assure you that if our friends feel the need to talk about Kate, it most certainly will be out of concern and the kindness of their hearts."

The serious moment lasted only a moment before they all, Kate included, erupted into laughter.

"Wow, Aunt Connie. I was really impressed there for a second." Kate walked over and put her arm around Constance, which at first seemed to surprise her. But then, slowly, Constance put her arm around Kate's waist and they continued to laugh.

When the oven timers announced that the food was ready, Patsy helped unload the dishes from the ovens and the ladies filled their plates. They refreshed their drinks and settled around the kitchen and family room to eat.

Kate found she was comfortable in the company of the women, and before she knew it, it was time to leave.

"Don't forget, ladies. Next week is at Patsy's house," Doctor Bellows announced. "We hope you will be there, Kate."

"I'd love to, Doctor Bellows. Thank you." Kate couldn't wait until it was Doctor Bellows' turn to host so she could see her house.

With Constance and Patsy loaded safely back in the car, Kate started the Range Rover and headed to Patsy's house.

"I'll call you in the morning," Patsy shouted to Constance as she disappeared into her house.

"This was a nice evening, Aunt Connie."

"I'm glad you had fun, dear."

Chapter Nine

THE NEXT DAY, KATE and Natalie made plans to meet at The Seagull at nine o'clock that evening. It was a gorgeous day, so Kate decided to take the Sunfish and go sailing. Kate sailed toward the little cove she loved to swim in as a child. She thought about taking a quick dip but the water was still too cold. Then she sailed to all the other spots she remembered from her childhood. Kate felt like a kid again. She discovered some new spots, too, and looked forward to making old spots out of them. Back home, she showered and had dinner with Constance before going to The Seagull. She noticed there were a lot of women at the bar. Natalie spotted her and waved her over.

"Big crowd here tonight, Nat. What's going on?"

"We do ladies' night on Saturday nights this time of year. There isn't normally such a big turnout, but Shannon put the word out to her friends." Natalie smiled as she looked around.

"Would it be safe to assume that most are gay?" Kate asked.

"The curious, as Shannon calls them."

"Ah, the straight ones looking for a little fun." Kate surveyed the room.

"Come on. I'll get you a beer."

Kate followed Natalie to the bar and grabbed one of the only empty stools.

"Glad to see you back." Shannon placed a beer in front of her.

"Thanks. And hi."

"Looks like you picked a good night." Shannon winked as she headed down the bar to fill another order.

Natalie pulled up a stool next to Kate. "So, how's it been going?"

"Good. Good. I've been busy."

"Getting along with Connie okay?"

"Yeah. It's been good so far."

"Glad to hear it." Natalie smiled and patted Kate's hand.

"I went to their potluck last night and that was fun."

"I hear it is. My mother used to go, but now she plays bridge on Friday night with another crowd."

After Kate and Natalie had been chatting for a while, Kate sensed someone was staring at her. When Kate turned and looked down the bar, a beautiful brunette was smiling at her. Kate smiled back. The brunette turned and said something to her friend before turning and smiling at Kate again. Kate took a good look at her. Tall, like Kate, the woman's skin was golden. She had quite the figure, and, Kate suspected, quite the attitude.

"Nat, do you know most of the women here?"

Natalie looked around. "Are you getting hit on already? Damn, I wish I was gay."

"Okay, after I pick up my beer, look over your shoulder to your left, about six bar stools down, and see if you know the brunette."

Natalie waited and then looked. "Yup. That's Faith Young, and from what I hear, she's a little more than curious but she's also married."

"The worst kind of curious." Kate sipped her beer.

"Why do they do that?" Natalie asked.

"Some are truly gay and never come out because they're expected to lead a certain lifestyle. Some are bi and just like being with both men and women."

Natalie shook her head. "I don't know. Seems to me you should just make up your mind and go with it."

Shannon appeared with another beer for Kate. "For you. From Faith. She's the brunette midway down the bar." Shannon gave Kate the 'be careful' look.

"Uh oh." Natalie squirmed in her seat.

"It's okay, Nat. This isn't the first time something like this has happened. I'll be right back."

Kate made her way down the bar. Just as Kate reached the group, Faith's friend signaled to Faith to turn around.

"Thank you for the beer."

"You're welcome," Faith purred. "I'm Faith Young." She put her hand out.

"I'm Kate Whitfield. Nice to meet you."

"This is my friend, Mary Beth."

Mary Beth extended her hand. "Hi."

"I haven't seen you around before." Faith sipped her cocktail.

"I'm here visiting my aunt."

"Well, I hope it's not a short visit."

"No. I'll be here for the summer, I think."

"Oh good. There are so many exciting things to do here on the island if you're interested."

Wow, this chick knows how to work it. But hey, what's a little flirting? "I'm always interested in exciting things."

"So, Kate Whitfield, what do you do for a living?"

"I'm a lawyer." Kate could see that that caught her interest.

"Really? Do you practice out here?"

"Not yet. I just left a practice in Manhattan." No sense in getting into details.

"I'm sure that you can find something out here or start your own business."

Natalie appeared beside Kate. "Okay Faith, I'm going to steal my friend back now."

"Would you ladies excuse me?" Kate added.

"Of course." Faith touched Kate's arm. "But make sure you come back and find me."

Kate and Natalie returned to their stools.

"Sorry, Nat. I just thought I'd have fun with her for a minute."

"Oh, it wasn't that," Nat assured her. "I just had to get you away from her."

"Why?"

"Because Shannon told me to."

As if on cue, Shannon joined them. "Sorry about that, Kate, but that Faith chick has caused a lot of problems for people I know."

"What kind?" Natalie's eyes lit up.

"She gets involved with them and won't leave them alone. Then, when the other person backs off, she proceeds to make their lives miserable."

"Wow," Natalie said with a gasp.

"That may be true, but nothing is going to happen. I mean, she's beautiful and sexy and all that, but—"

"There you go." Shannon cut her off, slapping her hand on the bar loud enough to make other patrons turn and look. "It's that kind of thinking that will get you in a whole lot of trouble."

"Nah, I mean, it'll be fine."

"Famous last words," Shannon said as she headed back to the kitchen.

For the next few hours, Kate chatted with some of the other patrons Shannon and Natalie introduced her to. Although Kate found some of the women attractive, she caught herself looking back at Faith on more than one occasion. Kate went to the bathroom and then headed out to the small porch overlooking a pond. The night air was cool and the stars were bright.

"Nice night." It was Faith. She stood close to Kate.

Kate was barely able to agree before Faith leaned in and kissed her hard. Kate was torn. Part of her said to take it easy, but the other part couldn't help but admit how hot this chick was. Kate kissed her back just as hard. She ran her hand up Faith's side and onto her breast. Faith gasped, and Kate went for more, sliding her hand under Faith's shirt and caressing her breast. It wasn't long before she unbuttoned Faith's jeans, and hungrily explored her. A few hot minutes later, Faith collapsed onto Kate's shoulder. After a few moments, Faith kissed Kate hard again, and pressed a piece of paper into Kate's hand

"Nice night," she said, before going back into the bar. Kate stood there another minute before looking at the piece of paper in her hand and discovering Faith's phone number. Kate went back inside.

"There you are," Natalie said from behind the bar. "You okay?"

"I'm fine. I just went out for some air."

"Want another beer?"

"Thanks, Nat, but I think I'll be heading home." After a quick hug, Kate made her way toward the door. Kate took one last look at Faith, who blew her a kiss. Kate smiled until she was out of The Seagull.

Chapter Ten

KATE SAT IN THE window seat of her room and looked out across the lawn. The early morning fog had just burned off, and the earth glistened in the mist left behind. She hadn't slept well and had been sitting there since five o'clock replaying in her mind everything that had happened since her arrival on the island, especially last evening. Finally, Kate got up, got dressed and went downstairs. She made herself a cup of tea and took it out on the patio.

She stared out over the water as she thought both troubling and calming thoughts. *What am I doing with my life? I feel like a kid on summer vacation. How do I manage to combine them both? How can I feel fulfilled yet not lose this sense of happiness I haven't felt since I was a kid?*

"Are you all right, dear?" Kate hadn't heard Constance come outside. Kate started to cry.

"There, there, dear," Constance said as she embraced Kate. Once Kate calmed down, Constance took Kate's cup. "I'll bring you some more tea."

Constance returned with a tray and let Kate prepare her own tea. The two sat in silence for a little while.

"I think I know what will do you a world of good," Connie said as she retrieved a key from the tray and passed it to Kate. It was the key to Arabella's Mercedes. "You haven't taken her out yet, dear, and I think you could use some time with your grandmother."

Kate nodded her head and stood up. "Thank you, Aunt Connie." Kate punched in the code and stood back as the door opened. She walked down the path to the garage, punched in the code and stood back as the door opened. After sliding into the driver's seat, she sat for a minute to catch her breath. She could almost hear her grandmother calling to her.

"Come along Kate. It's a beautiful day for a drive, and we don't want to miss a minute of it!"

Kate started the engine. Still sounded the same. She pulled slowly out of the garage. Constance stood at the top of the path smiling at her. Kate smiled back, waved, and headed up the driveway. At the road, she took a deep breath and headed north. It wasn't until after Kate pulled over to put the top down and her hair was dancing in the wind that she felt her grandmother's spirit. That never-give-up, be-all-you-can-be, live-life-to-the-fullest, don't-ever-let-anyone-or-anything-hold-you-back, you-know-what-you-want-now-go-get-it spirit. The more Kate thought about her grandmother, the faster she drove. *I can do this*, Kate told herself. *Whatever it is, I can do this.*

After rounding a curve a little faster than was safe, Kate slowed down and pulled off on one of the beach access roads. When she got to water, she parked the Mercedes and got out. She threw herself on the hood of the car and hugged it as if it truly was her grandmother. Kate would have felt silly had it not been for the renewed sense of confidence that was pulsing through her. She knew her grandmother was with her. She went and sat on the beach and made plans for her new life. When she was about to burst, Kate flew home to find her Aunt Connie.

"Aunt Connie! Aunt Connie," Kate shouted as she ran through the house.

Constance rushed down the back stairs. "What is it dear? Is everything okay?"

"Aunt Connie, who do we know that I could talk to about renting some office space?"

Constance tapped her forefinger on her chin for a moment. "Why, I think Lorraine Marshall could help us. I know her pretty well, and she runs a good real estate agency here."

"Can you call her and see if she might be in the office this morning?"

"Well, it is Sunday, but she is a good friend and maybe she'll be willing to help us today. Just what are we looking for?"

"Space to open my law office."

Constance smiled. "I'll get my phone book."

After what seemed an eternity, Constance finished the call and announced that Lorraine could see them at eleven. Perfect. That gave Kate just enough time to take a quick shower and change into more appropriate clothes.

"You'll go with me, Aunt Connie, won't you?"

Constance didn't hesitate. She grabbed her bag and headed toward the door. Looking back at Kate, she said, "Well let's go then, dear."

The two smiled at each other and left the house. When they got to the end of the path, Kate made her way to the Mercedes.

"Hop in, Aunt Connie. She's the inspiration for this trip, so she's what we're taking."

Constance hesitated for a second, but opened the door and slid in. She opened her purse and pulled out her kerchief. She looked at Kate through moist eyes. "I always feel her when I get in this car."

Kate grabbed Constance's hand for a second and smiled at her before starting the car and heading off.

Constance directed Kate to the real estate office. A short plump woman with dark brown hair greeted them when they arrived.

"Connie, you look wonderful. How are you?" Lorraine kissed Constance's cheek.

"Very well, Lorraine. Thank you. This is my niece, Kate."

"Nice to meet you." Kate shook Lorraine's hand.

"Please, have a seat and let's see what I can do for you. What exactly are you looking for?" Lorraine fussed around her desk for pen and paper.

"Well, I'd like to open a law office on the island. But I don't need anything extravagant, definitely something small. Maybe one office with a separate space for a reception area. I'm handy, so I don't mind if it needs some work."

Lorraine tapped her pen on the desk while Kate spoke.

"Okay, so you don't really need prime space. The rent would kill you just starting off, anyway. Maybe something over an existing business or a stand-alone off the beaten trail?" Lorraine picked up a listing sheet and pored over it. "All right. I have three spaces I can show you now if you'd like, to give you an idea of what's out there."

Kate looked at Constance, who nodded at her. "I have nothing planned until later in the day, dear. Let's go."

Lorraine led the way and Kate and Constance followed in the Mercedes. The first place they visited was so far off the beaten trail Kate felt no one would find it. They didn't go in. The second one was closer to town but had no parking. They didn't bother to go in it either. The third one, though, had potential. There was parking in the main downtown parking lot and the women walked only half a block before Lorraine stopped in front of a storefront two doors from The Seagull.

"Okay, ladies, follow me." Lorraine led them up a covered staircase that ran along the side of the building. She unlocked the door and held it open for Kate and Constance to enter. The space was bright and airy. Two large windows overlooked the main street and the harbor. The white wood paneling gave it a laidback beachy feel. Kate began making mental blueprints. *A half wall partition to the left of the door would be enough to hold a reception desk, and I could put up a wall over there to make a separate office.* The bathroom and small kitchen space were fine as they were.

Kate ran her foot along the floorboards, admiring the character of the wood grain.

"They're original," Constance said.

"This is very nice, Lorraine, but it's right in the middle of town." Kate looked at the realtor, who smiled back at her.

"It's lovely, dear," Constance said as she wandered around. "Look at this view."

"It was a clothing shop last summer, but they didn't come back this year," Lorraine explained.

"I'm sure they couldn't afford the rent." Kate stood in the middle of the room. "It would be perfect, though."

"Why don't you find out how much it is before you write it off?" Constance suggested.

"Aunt Connie, I have no income, and I'd spend my first few weeks setting up. Suppose I don't get any business the first month? I have savings, but I can't count on that to get me by forever."

"My dear, in order to be successful, sometimes you have to take a chance." Constance smiled at Kate with a twinkle in her eye.

Kate looked at Constance. "Okay, Lorraine, go ahead and hit me with it."

"Well, let me talk to the landlord and see what I can work out. She's a very generous woman, and I'm sure she'd be willing to be flexible."

"I guess it wouldn't hurt, but I'm pretty sure I won't be able to afford it."

Lorraine smiled and walked over to Constance. "Excuse me, Ms. Hilliard. I have a young lady who is interested in renting your space above the Green Pea on Cove Street. She'd like to open a law office and was wondering if you'd be willing to work out an agreement about the rent."

"Why, I do believe I might be able to work something out,"

Constance responded through a smile. "Would she like to meet with me now?"

Kate couldn't believe her ears. "You own this building, Aunt Connie?"

"Yes, dear."

"Wow. I had no idea."

"How would you, dear?"

"Aunt Connie, you know I can't pay full value for a space like this right now. And paying you less wouldn't be fair to you."

"Why don't we agree that you don't have to pay any rent until you have some clients, after which time we can work out terms that will be agreeable? Besides, you'll be making improvements to the space." Constance held out her hand. "Shall we shake on it, dear?"

Kate shook Constance's hand with a firm grip. "You have a deal."

"That's wonderful, ladies." Lorraine clapped her hands. "Why don't I leave you two to work everything out? Let me know if I can assist you further." Lorraine handed Constance the key.

"Thank you, Lorraine. I'll call you in the morning." Constance passed the key to Kate.

"Aunt Connie, that's twice today that you've handed me a key that has almost instantly changed my life."

"Now, I don't think we need to be that dramatic, dear."

For a moment, Kate saw the old Aunt Connie from her childhood, firm and distant, but the new Aunt Connie came right back.

"Besides, I think we may have had some help from above." Constance winked at Kate and linked her arm with Kate's. "Come dear. You were up early. It's Sunday. I say we go celebrate with some brunch. You'll have plenty to think over the next few days. For the afternoon at least, relax."

Kate agreed and ushered Constance to the door but stopped for a moment to take one last look at her new office before locking the door. Kate was ready for her new life, but first, brunch at the Rose and Thistle.

Chapter Eleven

CONSTANCE WAS RIGHT. KATE was busy the next few days. She called the super of her apartment in the City and asked him to make arrangements to pack and ship her law books and filing cabinets to the island. Her mother, who had returned from London, sent boxes Kate had stored at her house. Natalie and Shannon volunteered their help and helped clean and paint a few hours each morning before going to work at The Seagull and Kate called Dex to give him an update.

"What exactly are you going to do?" he asked.

Kate was sitting in the middle of the office floor sorting through boxes. "I'm going to open up and see who comes in and what they need."

"Wow. That's bold of you."

"Well, I have to start somewhere, and since I can't seem to make up my mind about what I want to do, I've decided that whatever it is will find me."

"Well, if you need anything, just call me."

"Don't think I won't."

Kate hung up, stood, and looked around. The built-in shelves were wonderful for holding all her books. One of Shannon's friends came and built the wall she wanted to separate the office from the reception area. Kate chose to keep all the woodwork white, so it only needed a fresh coat of paint. Everything else needed a good cleaning and some sprucing up and it was good to go. All that was left was furniture and she planned to shop for it once all the messy work was done. As she moved a box to the other side of the room, her cell phone vibrated and then rang. *Private number. Who could that be?*

"Hello?" Kate answered.

"I haven't been able to stop thinking about you since the other night."

Uh, oh. Faith. Kate felt chills run up her spine.

"Have you thought of me?" Faith asked.

"I have."

"Good. Why don't you come see me?"

Don't do it. "Well, I'm kind of busy."

"No. You need to come here and get busy."

"Where are you?" Kate looked at the side of a box to check its contents.

"Home."

Play this the right way. I know nothing about her, other than what I've been told. "Do you live alone?"

"I'm alone right now."

"Look, Faith, I don't want to get involved in anything that might be a problem."

"Why don't you come over, and I'll explain everything to you?"

I guess I could go hear what she has to say. Faith gave her directions to her home in East Hampton.

Kate arrived and was met by a ten-foot tall iron gate, but before she could buzz the call box, the gate opened. Right on the ocean, the house was a typical Hampton's beach house. Huge windows overlooked the water and brown clapboard weathered by the salt air. The door opened and Faith walked out to meet Kate at the car. After a brief hug, Faith guided Kate into the house.

"Just so you didn't think I planned on attacking you as soon as you arrived, I made us some lunch. It's on the patio by the pool house."

The two made their way through the house and the garden to the pool. There, under an umbrella, a table was set with wine and food. When they sat down, Faith poured them each a glass of wine.

"Beautiful place you have here," Kate said as she accepted her wine from Faith. "Live here by yourself?"

"Why don't we leave the boring details for some other time?" Faith touched her hand.

"Come on, Faith. You said if I came over you would answer my questions."

"Fine. I live here full time during the season and in Manhattan the rest of the year."

"And do you have a significant other?"

"I have a husband who is away most of the time. We have an understanding."

"Really? What kind of understanding?"

"Yes. Really. Basically, we have an understanding that we can do what we please when we're apart, but we appear together at numerous social events."

"So, you're unavailable for a real relationship, but open for fun and games."

Faith's expression told Kate that while that might be the truth, she wasn't usually called on it.

"Let's just say I don't have to worry about getting in trouble for my fun and games."

"What about the people you involve in your fun and games? Do they get in trouble?"

"Only if they cross me."

"Fair enough." Kate raised her glass.

Having satisfied her curiosity, Kate was content to chit chat and enjoy her lunch and wine. Not long after finishing their lunch, Faith gave Kate a tour of the pool house. Glass doors lined the wall that opened onto the pool. Lush beach furnishings decorated the room, and off to one side, as they finished the tour, was a bedroom.

"I was especially interested in showing you this room," Faith said as she took Kate's hand. "I think this time we should be a little more comfortable, don't you?"

Faith walked to the side of the bed and unbuttoned her blouse. She tossed it to the side and peeled her shorts from her hips. They glided down her legs and landed gently on the floor. As Faith stepped out of them, she motioned for Kate to join her.

Kate had been watching in silence, taking it all in. Faith certainly was gorgeous. She couldn't argue about that. Kate made her way to the side of the bed. Faith ran her hands up Kate's sides, stopping when her thumbs reached Kate's breasts. Kate took a deep breath and Faith ran her hands back down to the bottom of Kate's shirt and pulled it up over her head. Ever so slowly, Faith leaned in to kiss Kate, loosening Kate's shorts as she did. Kate returned Faith's kiss until she couldn't take it anymore and pushed Faith back onto the bed, falling with her. When Kate opened her eyes sometime later, she was lying across Faith's stomach. Faith ran her hand over Kate's back. Kate moaned.

"You certainly know how to please a woman," Faith said, smiling at Kate.

Kate smiled back. "You're not so bad yourself." It had been a long time since Kate had felt so satisfied.

"What time is it?" Kate asked.

"It's almost three-thirty."

"Wow. Time flies when you're having fun. I should get going."

"Take your time." Faith continued to rub Kate's back.

They stayed like that for a few more minutes before Kate slowly made her way up to Faith's lips and kissed her. They dressed and went back to the patio for one more glass of wine. Faith walked Kate out to her car where they shared one more kiss.

"See you soon?" Faith asked.

"You know the number. By the way, how did you get my number?" Kate said as she got in the car.

"There isn't anything I can't get once I want it."

"Good to know."

Kate watched Faith in the rearview mirror until she could no longer see her. *I could think of worse ways to spend an afternoon,* as the gate opened and poured her out into the road.

Chapter Twelve

"ALL RIGHT, DEAR, I think that's everything." Kate and Constance were almost finished loading the Range Rover. This week's potluck was at Patsy's. Kate almost had the office set up, so she felt up to a night with the ladies. Beginning Monday, she would be in the office full time. She had put a small announcement in the local paper advertising the opening of her general law office. With any luck, prospective clients would show up. Constance and Kate set off, but before they had a chance to start a conversation, they arrived at Patsy's.

"When were you here last, dear?" Constance asked as she removed bags from the car.

"Maybe a year or so ago. I came for a weekend with Gran and we came to Patsy's for lunch."

"Well, I think you will find it as stunning as ever."

They made their way to the front door. It swung open as they got there.

"Come on in, kid," Patsy bellowed. "And you too, Connie. Perfect timing."

Aunt Connie is right. Stunning is the word. Ever the designer, Patsy had taken great care to ensure her home looked like one from a magazine yet comfortable to live in. The views of the harbor spanned all the windows. It seemed that no matter where a person sat or where they looked, their focus would be on the view.

Kate followed Patsy into the kitchen. Just a few of the regulars had arrived so far, but since most of the ladies were in town, Patsy was expecting a big turnout for the evening. Kate said her hellos and helped with the set-up. Every time she turned around, another lady with a dish was making her way into the kitchen. Patsy handed Kate a glass of wine.

"So, how goes it?"

"I'll be open for business Monday morning."

"Good. I saw your ad. Nice. Not too much. Just enough." Patsy clinked her glass on Kates.

"I hope it's enough to get someone in the door."

"Oh, for Christ's sake, Marion. Just spoon it out and put it in the dish. Excuse me, kid." Patsy was off.

Kate took her glass of wine and went to the window. What a view. Kate's moment was disrupted by a commotion behind her. Someone was getting a huge reception. Kate smiled when she saw it was Doctor Bellows. *Why the excitement with her arrival?* She hadn't been away. In fact, Kate saw her at the last potluck. *Wait.* There was someone with her. Heads blocked Kate's view, but before she could get a better look, her cell phone vibrated. She slipped out to the patio.

"Hey there." A rush of energy pulsed through her.

"Hello there, lover. Why haven't you called me?"

"Sorry, Faith. I've been busy setting up my office since I last saw you last week. I haven't had any time for anything," Kate lied. She knew that playing with Faith was playing with fire. "Where are you?"

"I'm at some boring charity function in East Hampton. Why don't we meet some place?"

"I can't. I'm at a not so boring function."

"Well, what about tomorrow night? Want to meet at The Seagull?"

"Were you going anyway in case I can't make it?" Kate took a sip of wine.

"Yes. I'll most likely be there regardless."

"All right then. There's a chance I'll be there too."

"I'll be looking forward to it," Faith said as she hung up.

Kate congratulated herself for not committing to anything. Inside, the ladies were in full party mode. Kate made her way through the crowd to Constance and Patsy.

"There you are, dear. Everything all right?" "

"Fine, Aunt Connie. Just taking a phone call."

"Hot date?" Patsy said.

"Hot something," Kate said with a nod of her head.

Buzzing signaled that more food was ready. On cue, the ladies made their way to the kitchen to help themselves and find a spot to sit and eat. With so many people in the kitchen, Kate decided to wander around the first floor, taking in the décor. She stopped at the closed door of one of the bedrooms when she heard someone in the room talking.

"Look. I came out here because I thought it would be better if you left while I was gone. I don't care. I want you gone by the time I get back on Tuesday."

When she realized the call was ending, Kate made a dash into the next bedroom and pulled the door shut behind her just enough to avoid detection. Kate peeked through the opening to see who the speaker was. No luck. Whoever it was had already gone around the corner. *Wow. I hope I never have to go through something like that. Must be awful.*

The coast clear, Kate slid out from behind the door and made her way back to the party, inspecting faces as she went, trying to get an idea who was on the phone. She checked the ladies in the kitchen to see if a new face had appeared. *Well, I suppose if you're upset you aren't going to want to eat.* She went to the living room. Defeated, Kate went back to the kitchen to get her plate of food.

Patsy waved Kate over to the large kitchen table. Settling in, Kate spotted Doctor Bellows in the sunroom in what looked like a private conversation. *Who is she talking too?* Kate couldn't see and it was killing her. She strained to see around the chair that was blocking her view. Before she realized it, she was practically in Patsy's lap.

"Look, kid, if you want something off my plate, just ask." Patsy laughed.

"Sorry, Patsy. I was trying to see who Doctor Bellows is talking to. Can you see who it is?"

"Ellie? Where is she?"

"Out in the sunroom."

Patsy stood up and looked to the sunroom.

"Patsy, no," Kate gasped.

"Well, how else am I supposed to see? Oh, that's Ellie's granddaughter. She arrived a few days ago." Patsy munched on celery, waving the stalk around in between bites. "She's a doctor like her grandmother and practices in Manhattan. Don't ask me what type of medicine she practices. Couldn't tell you if I had to save my life."

Kate was still trying to see when Constance and some of the other ladies joined them at the table. When Kate got a chance to look again, the sunroom was empty. Twice before the night was over Kate made her way around the crowd looking for Ellie and her granddaughter but with no luck. *Why the hell am I so interested in this anyway?* Kate finally asked herself. *Was it what I heard on the phone, or just because I'm curious about what Ellie's granddaughter is like?*

***

On the way home, Constance told Kate of plans she had made for the following morning.

"Let me get this straight, the ladies want to spend the day at the cove and they want to get there by boat?" Kate asked.

"That's right, dear."

Kate pulled the Range Rover up to the garage and turned off the engine.

"Aunt Connie, I don't mean to be disrespectful, but I worry about some of those ladies walking and driving let alone powering a boat."

"No, dear. They have crews for that."

"Oh, and do you have a crew?"

"Why, of course, dear. That would be you."

Chapter Thirteen

THE FOLLOWING MORNING, KATE made her way to the marina to pick up Belle's boat. Boat. The term made Kate laugh. *Call it what it is, Aunt Connie. A yacht.* Kate slipped the Mercedes into a spot near the pier and made her way to where Belle's Water Lily was docked. Kate sighed as she walked alongside the vessel. *What wonderful times we have had on that boat.* Kate smiled to herself.

"Welcome aboard," someone bellowed from above.

Kate looked up, shielding her eyes from the sun. "Hello?"

"What's the matter, Kate? Don't you remember me?"

"Cap? Oh my god, Cap. Is that you?"

"Well, who the hell else do you think it would be?" Captain John Haywood bounded down the gang plank and onto the pier. After sweeping Kate up in a bear hug, Cap gave her the once over. "Look at you, still the skinniest deckhand I ever had."

"Oh, Cap, it's so good to see you. I didn't think you still did this."

"Naw. Can't get rid of me that easy. What in the hell else would I be doing anyway?"

Captain John had been the boat captain since Belle and Edward bought Belle's Water Lily. In fact, rumor was that he came as a condition of the sale. Whether that story was to be believed or not, it was true that Captain John had been there from the start and had sailed Belle and Edward anywhere they wanted to go for many years. *He must be pushing eighty,* Kate thought as they boarded the vessel and headed up to the bridge, but he was still as big and ornery as he was when Kate was a kid.

"What's this I hear about the ladies wanting to go on a day cruise?"

"Those are my instructions, Cap. Get down here and make sure everything is ready for when they arrive."

"There's not much for you to do. The servers and bartender have already loaded the food and drinks and we're all gassed up and ready to go."

No sooner had the words left his lips than the sound of voices echoed down the pier. "Yup, looks like they are headed our way." Cap shook his head. "Come on, Kate. Let's go sound them aboard."

"Hello, ladies, and welcome aboard," Cap bellowed, "but this time, let's behave ourselves, shall we? I don't want to have to throw any of you pretty ladies overboard." Cap winked at Kate. The ladies giggled.

"Aunt Connie, I thought they were taking their own boats out?" Kate said.

"Yes, dear, that was the original plan, but after some phone calls this morning, we decided that it would be more fun to be all on one boat."

"And I take it we are not going to the cove since it would've been easier to take the smaller boats there?"

"That's correct, dear. Today we are sailing around the island and to points unknown." Constance widened her eyes for dramatic effect.

Kate laughed. "Is everyone here?"

"Yes. We made sure we counted everyone while we were in the parking lot."

"All righty then, Cap, let's get this show on the road."

Cap signaled to the dock hands to untie the ropes and Kate followed him to the bridge. He maneuvered the yacht away from the dock and, in minutes, Belle's Water Lily was headed into the bay. Kate stayed on the bridge for a while taking in the beauty of the island from the water, but the sound of laughter below finally roused her enough to go see what was happening.

Patsy handed her a glass of champagne. "Come on, kid. Come join the party."

The ladies didn't waste time getting their party on. Champagne corks popped left and right, and food was everywhere. Kate leaned against a column and wandered off in thought for a moment. Parties like this were the memories she had of this boat. Her grandparents, parents, and friends out on the water for a weekend or longer vacation. It was nice to see people enjoying something that her grandmother loved so much.

"Are you all right?" a voice beside her asked.

Kate was startled and wiped her eyes. She hadn't realized she was crying. "Yes, I, ah, yes, thank you. I was just reminiscing." Kate turned to focus on the owner of the voice. The woman was about Kate's height with shoulder length blonde hair and deep blue eyes that seemed to reach into her soul. She was striking.

"I don't believe we've met," the blonde said.

Still blinking through her tears, Kate held out her hand. "I'm Kate Whitfield. Constance Hilliard is my aunt."

"I'm Lane Bellows. Eleanor Bellows is my grandmother. Nice to meet you."

The women stood there shaking hands in silence for a moment before they realized their hands were still linked. They laughed and released their hands.

"I'm sorry. Have we ever met before?" Kate asked.

"I don't think so. I know your aunt, and I knew your grandmother, but I don't think we were ever out here at the same time. Funny. You would think we would have met at some point."

Kate did not respond.

Lane broke the silence. "Well, we've met now."

"Can I get you a drink?" Kate motioned toward the bar.

"That would be great."

"One of these?" Kate pointed to her glass.

Lane nodded and they made their way to the bar.

"A toast." Kate held up her glass. "To new friends."

"To new friends," Lane agreed. They clicked glasses.

"So, how long are you visiting?" Kate asked as they walked to the boat railing.

"Probably until Tuesday. I have patients scheduled for the rest of week."

"Ah, that's right. You're a doctor like your grandmother."

"Someone's been talking about me."

Kate was drawn in by Lane's soft and flowing laughter. She flashed back to the night before and the fuss that was made when Doctor Bellows came in, the woman having an argument on the phone, and Doctor Bellows comforting someone in the sunroom. It must have been Lane. *What was her story? Was she breaking up with someone?* Kate pulled herself together and, fudging the truth a little, kept the conversation going.

"Yes. I believe your name came up at one of the potlucks. Have you been to one yet?"

"Actually, we stopped by briefly last night," Lane said. *Ah, yes. I just figured that out*, Kate thought. She let Lane continue. "We had some other plans, but my grandmother was afraid she'd miss something and insisted we at least pass through."

Better change the subject. Kate didn't want to let on that she had heard any of the phone conversation. "What type of medicine do you practice?"

"I'm a cardiologist."

"Wow, that's pretty cool. Do you operate on people?" Kate was impressed.

"No, but I thought about it at one time."

"Really? I can't imagine doing that."

"Well, I think that was my problem. I mean, I've been in the operating room, and I still go into the operating room, but the thought of actually doing the operation is where I fell short. So, what do you do?" Lane sipped her champagne as the wind gently caressed her bangs. Kate had to stop herself from reaching out to brush them out of her eyes.

"I'm a lawyer."

"Malpractice?" There was that laugh again.

"I used to practice corporate law, but now I practice general law. I just finished setting up an office in town."

"Really? Out here?"

"Yes. I was with a firm in the City—that's a whole other story and a long one—but the bottom line is that I came out here to think about where I want to be. Turns out that, for now, it's here." Kate smiled. She was happy with her decision. Kate felt a pang of panic as she added, "Hopefully I'll get some clients."

"I'm sure you will.

Distracted by Lane's gentle touch on her arm, Kate barely heard what Lane said. "Sure. Thanks."

"Hey, you two." Patsy joined them at the railing. "Do you ladies need an introduction?"

"No," they answered together.

Kate added, "We took care of that, but thank you."

"I didn't think you two had met, but it's surprising you haven't. God knows we've all known each other since the dinosaurs. All right then, continue." Patsy turned back to the other ladies, winking at Kate as she did.

"Is your family here with you? Husband? Kids?" Might as well get the whole story, Kate decided.

"No. I'm not married, and I don't have any children."

"Some day?" Kate asked.

"Yes, I think one day I would like to have kids. Of course, it's all about finding the right person to raise a family with."

"Ah yes, that elusive right person."

"So, you're looking too?"

Kate was certain she heard sadness in Lane's voice. "I haven't been looking. For the longest time, it was all about my career, and I gravitated toward short-term, no-complication types of relationships…It worked at the time."

"And now?"

"Now, I'm not so sure what I'm looking for. I mean, I'm still struggling trying to find my way."

Wow, did I just say all that? Kate surprised herself. She hadn't thought much about her relationship status recently. She was having fun with Faith. She was sure that wasn't going anywhere, but for now, maybe that was all she needed.

"Well, I guess we'll both have to wait and see what life has planned." Lane held up her glass. "To finding out."

"To finding out."

"I haven't been very hungry lately, but this salt air is making me want to eat. How about you?" Lane looked at the food trays the servers had placed on the tables. The other ladies were helping themselves.

"Lots going on in life?" Kate asked.

"Yes. You might say it's been a little stressful. But I feel comfortable today."

"I'm glad to hear it. Let's check out what's on the menu."

"Lead the way."

Lane followed Kate to the food. They filled their plates and made their way to one of the tables. Kate got them more champagne.

"Too much more of this and I might end up overboard." Lane laughed.

"Don't drink much?"

"No. I usually have such a hectic patient schedule I'm forced to restrict myself to one glass of wine with dinner or per event. Unless, of course, I'm on vacation or have a rare long weekend off."

"I thought doctors were always on vacation. You know, late to the office, early out of the office, golf on Wednesday. That's the kind of schedule doctors had when I was growing up."

"I think that comes with experience. Us newbies have to earn that right."

"Well, I have an idea. Since you're on a long weekend, how about meeting me at The Seagull tonight? You can have as many or as few drinks as you like. I'll pick you up and take you home."

"Why, that's quite an offer. I mean, you don't even know me."
Showing a gesture of innocence, Lane put her hand on her heart.

"Come on. It'll be fun. And who knows? Maybe you'll meet someone."

"Okay. I'll take you up on your offer, but believe me, the last thing I want to do is to meet anybody."

Chapter Fourteen

THE OUTING ENDED WITH the boat safely docked and all the ladies accounted for. Constance made it an early evening, taking a cup of tea and a book to relax in bed.

After a quick nap, Kate took a shower and got ready to pick Lane up at nine o'clock. It didn't take long to get on the road to Doctor Bellows' house. She had a good idea where it was, but since she had never been there, she took her time. She spotted the house number on a large boulder and turned down the long, lantern-lit driveway. Kate hopped out of the car and headed for the door. When she got to the porch, she realized there were two front doors. They were solid wood and massive. In the center of each hung a large wrought iron knocker and on each side, large lanterns. Kate pushed the doorbell. A melody of gentle bells responded. When one of the doors opened, Kate caught her breath. The soft lights behind Lane made her seem as though she was glowing.

"Hi, there. Would you like to come in for a tour or save that for some other time?" Lane asked.

"How about we save it for another time?"

"All right. I'm ready to go." Lane stepped outside, but Kate, who was still caught up in Lane's glow, didn't move. After an awkward moment, Kate stepped to the side and let Lane go ahead of her.

"Nice car. That lawyer's pay can't be too bad." Lane ran her hand along the door of the Range Rover.

"Okay. I'm embarrassed and since no one's asked me about it, I guess I haven't come up with a clever answer." Kate opened the door for Lane and went around to the driver's side and got in.

"Why do you need a clever answer?"

"Because my Aunt Connie bought it for me." Kate covered her eyes.

"That's nice." Lane buckled her seat belt.

"Come on, you know you want to make fun of me."

"No, I don't. My family has money too, and sometimes the gifts they give you aren't what others are used to. I understand how it can be embarrassing."

"So, how did your family embarrass you?" Kate asked as she pulled onto the main road.

"It really wasn't a problem when I was younger because I was in private school and the other kids had the same lifestyle I did. It was once I got into medical school and into relationships that it was sometimes a problem."

"What do you mean?"

"Some people made fun of the way I lived or was brought up, and others took advantage of it."

"So, some people found your lifestyle appalling, and others wanted to experience it for themselves."

"Didn't you have that problem?"

"Not really. My grandmother and aunt were the ones with all the real money. My mom's an artist and my dad's a doctor. Our lives were pretty quiet."

"Wow, your mom's an artist? Would I know her work?"

"I don't know, maybe. Her name is Morgan Whitfield."

Lane gasped. "What? Your mother is Morgan Whitfield?"

"Yes." Kate never had a reaction like this to her mother's name.

"Oh, my god." Lane raised her hand to her mouth.

Kate pulled into the parking lot at the Seagull. She shut the car off and looked at Lane. "I take it you know of her?"

Lane nodded her head. "Know her? I have one of her paintings hanging over my bed. It's one of my favorite things in the world."

"Seriously?"

"Seriously."

Kate and Lane got out of the car in silence and headed in to The Seagull. They made their way through the crowd to the bar.

Shannon greeted them. "How are you, Kate? What can I get you and your lovely friend this evening?"

"Hi, Shannon. I'd like you to meet Lane."

Shannon extended her hand across the bar.

"Nice to meet you, Lane. What can I get you?"

Lane seemed at loss for an answer and looked at Kate.

Kate remembered what Lane said on the yacht. "If you have beer, you can have more than one, and you probably won't have a problem.

If, on the other hand, you have wine or a drink, you can only have one."

Lane leaned close to Kate. "What are you having?"

"Beer."

Lane turned to Shannon.

"Nice to meet you too, Shannon. I'll have whatever Kate's having."

"Okay, ladies, I'll be right back."

"There you go. Come on, have a seat and let's get comfortable." Kate pulled out two bar stools.

Shannon returned with two mugs of beer.

Lane watched Kate take a sip and then lifted her glass to her lips.

Kate giggled. "You've got a little foam action going on up." Without hesitation, she leaned over and gently wiped off the foam from Lane's upper lip.

"Thank you."

For a second, Kate could have sworn Lane blushed.

"Hey, Kate. How are you?" Natalie pushed her way between Kate and Lane. Without waiting for Kate to respond, she turned to Lane. "I know you. You're Lane Bellows."

"Yes, I am."

"And you know me. I'm Natalie Brewster."

Kate could tell from Lane's expression that at that moment she had no idea who Natalie was.

"Tell her, Kate." Natalie turned and looked at Kate.

"She's Natalie Brewster," Kate confirmed. Natalie grinned and turned back to Lane.

"Come on. We had swim class together, and you came to some of my birthday parties."

"Oh. Natalie Brewster. Of course, I know you."

Kate could tell Lane was still searching her memory.

"Oh, my god. This is so cool us all being together again." Natalie did a little dance. "Let me get your next round." In a flash, she was behind the bar.

Kate whispered to Lane, "Do you remember her?"

"I think so. We did hang out, I think."

"Don't worry, I'm sure Natalie will remind you of everything."

Kate spied Faith coming in the door. *Oh shit, I forgot about her.*

Faith and the friend she was with took two stools at the far end of the bar near the windows. Once seated, Faith spun around on the stool checking the crowd. Kate adjusted her stool so that Lane blocked Faith's view of her, for now anyway.

Lane smiled as she looked around the bar. She looked back at Kate. "This is really nice. It's been a while since I've been out like this."

"Like this?"

"I mean just relaxing, not a charity function, not a work function, not a date kind of thing."

"Ah, back to the relationship kind of thing. Do you date much?"

"Sorry, girls, I got delayed in the kitchen." Natalie leaned across the bar. "Do you two remember my twelfth birthday party when I had the piñata? Isn't that where you met each other?

"You know, Natalie, I don't think Kate and I met out here before today," Lane said.

"I'm going to go through some pictures. I'm sure that somewhere along the line you met."

Lane took a small breath and opened her mouth to speak but was interrupted.

"I thought I saw you over here." Faith kissed Kate on the cheek. "Didn't you see me come in?"

"No." Kate felt her cheeks start to blush.

"Well, when you're done here, come on over." She tugged at Kate's sleeve and smiled at Lane and Natalie as she went back to her seat.

Natalie jumped on Kate. "Okay, what's going on?"

"Who was that?" Lane asked.

"Seriously, Kate, something's going on with you two." Natalie leaned over the bar to get a better look at Kate.

"Who was that?" Lane repeated.

"Nothing is going on, Nat. We just had a conversation the other night and—"

"And that's not good, Kate. You know about her, and, believe me, I checked with Shannon, and she is nobody you want to get involved with."

"I'm not involved. I only met her for lunch once."

"You met her for lunch?" Natalie's forehead crinkled.

"I know what I'm doing, Nat, and even if I don't, it's not a big deal. Nothing is going to happen."

"Be careful, Kate."

"I will."

"Okay, now that you have that settled, may I ask again who that was?" Lane asked Kate, but Natalie jumped in before Kate could answer.

"Her name is Faith Young. She's married, from the Hamptons, and has girl crushes that usually end in someone getting hurt. And it's not usually Faith." Natalie looked at Kate to make a point.

Kate shrugged her shoulders.

"I have it on good authority from Shannon, my bartender, that she usually fixates on someone when she is here for the summer, and then when she heads back to Manhattan she finds someone else there to occupy her."

"So, this is a problem because?" Lane sipped her beer.

"Because she might be fixating on Kate this summer."

"Kate's a big girl. If she finds Faith attractive and wants to be a part of whatever Faith has going on, she knows what she's getting into." Lane came to Kate's defense.

"Thank you, Lane."

"On the other hand, if Faith is anything like some of the women I've met over the years, Kate might be in for quite a ride." Lane took another sip of her beer.

Natalie sighed and went into the kitchen.

Kate crossed her arms and squinted at Lane.

"Yes? May I help you with something?" Lane took a long swallow of her beer.

"Well, I'll be darned. I guess my gaydar isn't working properly."

"Meaning?"

"Meaning you're as gay as I am."

"Ah, yeah." Lane put her beer on the bar.

"So, why didn't you say something? All this dancing around relationships and finding the right one?" Kate emphasized 'the right one' with air quotes.

"What dancing around? We don't know each other that well, and I don't share everything right away."

"I can't believe you didn't say something to give me a hint at least. It's kind of the unspoken rule, no?"

"What are you talking about?"

"I mean when you find common ground with someone, you share it."

"Eventually."

"What do you mean, 'eventually?'

"You could be some kind of nut who pretends to be someone you're not, and then causes trouble." Lane waved her hand in the air.

"What the hell does that mean?"

"I mean in my position, with my career, I'm very careful about who knows what about my life. There are people that might have a problem knowing that their cardiologist is a lesbian."

"I can understand that, but not when you just met another lesbian who you know would protect your privacy."

"Well, again, that comes down to finding out if you're a nut or not. Why are you getting so upset about this?"

Kate stopped and thought about it for a moment. *Why am I getting so fired up?* "I'm not really sure." She stared at her beer for a moment. "I think I need some air." She got up and went out on the patio. She took a few deep breaths as she gazed at the pond. Suddenly, arms wrapped around her waist and a warm breath whispered in her ear.

"Shall we recreate the night we met?"

Kate turned and kissed Faith.

"Now that's the greeting I was waiting for. I've missed you."

"Sorry, Faith. I've just been busy trying to get things in order."

"That's okay, babe, as long as we get together soon. I'm staying at a small hotel on the island tonight. Why don't you come meet me?"

Kate ran her hands down Faith's back and kissed her neck.

"Tell me where you are staying, and the room number, and let me know when you leave. I'll be a half an hour behind you." She kissed Faith again and went back inside. She stopped short as she caught sight of Lane dancing like crazy in front of the jukebox. Kate walked up behind Lane, watching as Lane moved her hips to the music. The way Lane's jeans hugged her ass distracted her for a moment before she touched Lane on the shoulder.

Lane spun around, beer in hand.

"I just love this song, don't you?"

"Yeah, it's great.

The look on Lane's face became serious.

"It's so rare that I get to be so carefree without getting in trouble." Her eyes filled with tears.

"No, no, no. Don't be upset. You can dance your heart out. In fact, if you want to dance, I'll dance with you."

"You will?"

"Of course. Why not? As you said, it's a great song."

"Now it's over."

"Well, pick another song and let's dance."

Lane's smile widened as she turned and chose another song from the jukebox. They laughed their way through the dance and, when it was over, went back to the bar.

"Thank you, Kate." Lane settled on her bar stool.

"My pleasure. Any time you want to dance, just say the word."

"I will."

Kate felt uneasy as she asked. "Can I ask what upset you before? Didn't you go out and dance with your last girlfriend?"

"No. I was supposed to be in control and hide my feelings and not embarrass myself or her."

"Wow, that's a tall order. Didn't she like to do things and have fun?"

"I've come to find out that she had no problem doing things with the girl she was cheating on me with that she wouldn't do with me."

Shannon brought over two more beers.

"Thanks." Kate handed Lane a beer. "I'm sorry, Lane. I had no idea."

"How would you? We just met. We don't know much about each other."

"I know you like to dance."

Lane laughed. "I do."

"Look, Lane. I know what you said about being a doctor and being private in that respect, but in your private life you should be able to be yourself and do what you want. If you're in a relationship, isn't the other person supposed to encourage you and help you grow?"

Lane grabbed Kate's hand. "Whoever gets you will be one lucky woman."

"I don't know about that. I just know that's what I want in a relationship and maybe that's why I'm not in one yet. I haven't found anyone who will take care of me like that or who I want to take care of like that." *Hmmmm, is that how I really feel?*

"Excuse me, Kate. I have to go to the ladies' room." Lane tripped as she stood up and fell against Kate. As she caught herself and tried to stand back up, her cheek brushed Kate's, their lips nearly touching. "Oh my gosh, I'm so sorry."

"It's okay." Kate held Lane's arm to steady her before Lane walked away. Kate watched her go, once more admiring her new friend's shapely ass.

Shannon leaned over the bar in front of Kate. "Damn, she sure is pretty."

Shannon didn't stick around for Kate to respond, but she wouldn't have argued with her anyway. Kate thought about the soft outline of Lane's face.

"Old Pond Inn, Room 112. See you soon."

Kate looked around but Faith was gone. *Did I imagine that?* She checked her watch. *Damn, how am I going to do this?* She felt bad. Lane was having fun and Kate liked hanging out with her, but she wanted to go have some fun too. *Okay, I need to be tactful. If Faith has to wait a little while, so be it.*

"I didn't realize it was getting so late. Do you mind if we finish our beers and go? I don't want to spoil your evening. You can take me home and can come back," Lane said when she returned from the bathroom.

Perfect. Kate couldn't have planned that better. "Shannon brought us two more beers. How about we finish them and then I'll take you home?"

"Great."

The two women engaged in lighthearted conversation while they finished their beers. There was little conversation on the ride to Lane's place.

"Thanks so much for taking me out tonight, Kate. I really needed it."

"Not a problem. It was fun. We'll have to do it again sometime." Kate smiled at the thought.

Lane reached for her purse but stopped and turned, grabbed Kate by her collar, pulled her to her, and kissed her. Kate started to push her back, but realized she'd wanted to kiss Lane all night, especially after watching her move to the music. The kiss made her realize how much she wanted Lane. Kate was attracted to her—the way she looked, the way she smelled, the way she felt.

Lane pulled back and looked at Kate. "I'm sorry. Should I not be doing this?"

Kate held Lane's face in her hands. "At this moment, you can do whatever you want."

Lane kissed her again and then stopped again.

"I think I have the shifter up my ass, so we can either take this in the backseat or you can come inside."

"What about your grandmother?"

"She went to the City to see a show and is staying overnight with friends. I have the house to myself."

"Well then, what the hell are we doing out here? Let's go inside."

They raced inside and were all over each other as they made their way up the stairs.

"Let's take it easy," Kate laughed. "We don't want to hurt ourselves on the stairs and never make it to the bedroom."

Leaving a trail of clothes behind them, they finally fell together on Lane's bed. They spent the rest of the evening wrapped around each other, harmonizing soft caresses and passionate intensity. When Kate opened her eyes the next morning, she didn't recognize her surroundings. The previous night's adventures came back to her and she realized she was alone in the bed. She sat up and looked around. The room was beautiful, decorated in shades of yellow. Floor to ceiling windows overlooked the harbor.

Kate drew the blankets up to her chin, laid back on the pillows, and closed her eyes. Then it hit her and her eyes flew open. *Shit. Faith.* She had forgotten all about Faith. *Oh, well. I'll come up with something.* The door opened and Lane came in carrying a tray.

"Good morning."

"Good morning to you." Kate sat up.

"I wasn't sure what you liked in the morning, so I made both coffee and tea."

"How thoughtful. Thank you. Tea, please."

Lane set the tray on the table next to the bed. Lane handed Kate a cup and took one for herself as she sat on the edge of the bed.

"Kate, I hope that I didn't...I mean, I hope...I hope I didn't overstep my bounds or do anything that made you uncomfortable."

Kate set her tea on the night stand and slid over to hold Lane. "Last night was nothing short of fantastic, so not another word."

They kissed and then Lane made herself comfortable on the bed next to Kate. They drank their tea in silence for a minute before Kate burst into laughter.

Lane looked at her. "What?"

"I was just thinking that for someone who gave me the impression she might be shy, you sure went for it last night. Guess I was wrong."

Lane smiled with satisfaction. "When someone makes you feel confident, it can change the way you think about things. Not to mention I had a few beers.

"Whatever the reason I had a really nice evening and I think that anytime you need help with your confidence, you give me a call." Kate ran her finger down Lane's arm.

"I might just take you up on that." Lane moved over and kissed Kate. Passions flared again.

An hour later, Kate finished her tea. "I think I should be going."

"I stopped on the staircase and brought our clothes up before I made the coffee and tea. The bathroom is through there." Lane pointed to a doorway.

Lane was dressed and waiting for Kate when she came back to the bedroom. Together they made their way to Kate's car.

"When are you going back to the City?" Kate opened the car door.

"Tuesday morning."

"Can I take you to dinner tomorrow night?"

"That would be nice." Lane stepped in close to Kate

Kate kissed her. "I'll call you later."

Kate got in her car and waved as she pulled away. At the end of the driveway, she checked her phone. Three missed calls and one message. *This isn't going to be good.*

Chapter Fifteen

IT WAS A LITTLE BEFORE eight a.m. when Kate got to the house. There was no sign of Aunt Connie as she headed through the kitchen and up the back stairs. Just as she sat down on the bed, there was a knock on the door.

"Everything all right, dear?"

Think fast. "Just fine. Aunt Connie. I had a little too much to drink last night and crashed at Natalie's. I should have called." *Remember to tell Natalie.*

"That's quite all right, dear. There are enough people on this island who know us. In the event of an emergency, I'm sure I would be contacted immediately. Come down when you are ready."

Kate hadn't thought about how staying out all night would affect her aunt. It had been years since she had to explain herself to anyone. But she would have to be more considerate. After all, she was staying in Constance's home. Kate lay back on the bed. She had to figure out how to deal with Faith. *No sense in calling her now, it's too early.* Kate's phone rang. It was Faith. *Apparently not. Shit. Think fast.*

"Hi, there," Kate said when she answered the phone.

"Really? I waited up for you and called you and left you a message and all I get is 'Hi, there'?" Faith sounded furious.

"Ah, honey, that means you must care." Kate adjusted the pillow to sit up.

"Don't give me that bullshit. Where were you?"

"Look, Faith, I'm sorry. I was on my way over when my aunt called and said she wasn't feeling well. I came back to the house and called her doctor. I got so upset I forgot to call and by the time he got here and saw her and we got her settled in, well, I just passed out." *Whew.*

Silence.

"Faith? Really. I'm sorry. Are you still there? I can come over now."

Please say no.

"Are you sure that's what happened?"

Damn. Does she know? No, she couldn't.

"Of course, it is. And I feel really bad. You know I was looking forward to seeing you."

"Well, you're out of luck now. I'm checking out in a few minutes and going to brunch with some friends in East Hampton."

"When can I see you?" Kate would know in a moment how much trouble she was in.

"Not sure when I'll be back on the island, but I'll call you and we'll see what we can work out."

"Great. And Faith, I really am sorry."

"Just don't disappoint me again," Faith said as she hung up.

Kate stared at her phone for a second before setting it on the nightstand. *Dodged that bullet,* she thought as she drifted off to sleep. She awoke an hour later and headed down to the kitchen. She was happy to see a platter of scones on the kitchen counter. She put the kettle on to make some tea.

As she waited for the kettle to boil, she looked out the window towards the patio. Aunt Connie and Ellie looked like they were having a serious and animated discussion. Hand gesturing accompanied by head holding. *That can't be good. What is going on? Did they know about her and Lane? Wait, didn't Lane say her grandmother went into the City and was staying overnight? Did she come home early and see me leave? But why would that be such a big deal?*

"Yoo-hoo!" Patsy announced herself on the way from the front of the house.

"What are you doing coming in that way?" Kate nearly jumped out of her skin but recovered quickly and motioned for Patsy to be quiet.

"What's going on, kid?" Patsy crept up beside her and looked out the window. "Oh."

"Oh? What does that mean, oh?" Kate whispered.

"Nothing. I mean, I don't know." Patsy was stalling and Kate knew it.

"Come on Patsy. That looks like a serious discussion going on out there."

"Look, kid. No one tells me anything. Why are you being so nosy? You hiding something?"

"Me? No, but you always know what's going on."

Kate and Patsy watched Ellie stand up. They ducked away from the window.

"Is she coming in?" Patsy tried to peek.

Kate had a better angle. "Nope. Looks like she's leaving."

"What's Constance doing?

"I can't see."

Just then, the mudroom door opened and Constance entered the kitchen. Kate and Patsy scattered, trying to look nonchalant. Constance looked at them. "Good morning."

"Morning, Aunt Connie." Kate grabbed the teapot.

"Morning, Constance." Patsy grabbed a scone.

"Why don't you bring the tea and scones out to the patio, dear? Patsy and I will get the plates." Constance took some plates from the cabinet and went back to the patio and Patsy followed her.

Kate waited a moment before looking out the window. She couldn't see the women's faces as they made their way to the table, but she could tell that Patsy was the one doing all the talking. When they sat down, she saw Aunt Connie finally get a word in, shaking her head all the while.

What is that all about? Kate picked up the tea kettle and plate of scones and joined them.

"So, kiddo, I hear someone had a great night." Patsy smirked as she bit into a scone.

"Yes. I had a little too much fun and thought it best not to drive." Kate watched Aunt Connie for any expression that might give away how much she knew about Kate's adventures the night before. But Aunt Connie's face didn't change.

"Any plans for the day, dear?" Constance sipped her tea.

"No. I have some notes I want to make for when I go into the office tomorrow, but that's about it."

"Any bites yet?" Patsy asked.

"Not yet, but I'm going to run another ad in the paper this week."

"By the way, dear, Richard Brodman is coming to see me Wednesday afternoon. Do you think you might be able to join us here at the house for lunch?

"That would be fine, Aunt Connie. I hope he brings Dex."

"Am I invited?"

"Yes, Patsy dear, you are invited as well. Lunch will be served at 12:30. Please be sure to be here by noon," Constance said as she reached for a scone.

Chapter Sixteen

MONDAY WAS ANOTHER quiet day in the office. Kate contacted the newspaper office about running another advertisement, this time offering a free consultation for new clients. Just before she headed home, she called Lane to confirm their date. Since weather reports said it was going to be a stunning evening, Kate chose the Lamplight Restaurant for dinner. Overlooking the bay, it would offer a beautiful view of the moonrise.

As Kate signaled to turn into the Bellows' driveway, Ellie pulled out and waved at her. *Guess she's going out for the evening too.* Lane came from the back of the house as Kate pulled up. Dressed in a sleeveless, orange sherbet-colored dress with a matching shawl, she looked like a summer goddess. Kate got out of the car and walked toward her.

"You look gorgeous." She kissed Lane on the cheek.

"Why, thank you. You look lovely yourself."

Anticipating it might get cool once the sun set, Kate had picked a turquoise blue, three-quarter sleeve dress. It was practical, but still sexy.

"Well, I wouldn't want to disappoint you."

"So far so good."

"Shall we?" Kate motioned toward the car.

At the restaurant, they opted to sit outside on the terrace. Colorful flowers filled the plant boxes and candles in little jars danced in a light breeze. And, if it got too cool, there were outdoor heaters the staff could light.

The waiter returned with the bottle of wine they ordered and, after filling their glasses, left them to peruse the menu.

"So, do you have a busy week of patients waiting for you?" Kate asked after she tasted the wine.

"Yes. I also have some personal things to take care of that I'm not looking forward to."

"Everything all right?"

"It will be. I recently ended a relationship. She was cheating on me." Lane took a sip of wine.

"You mentioned that."

"I gave her until I get back tomorrow to be out of my apartment. I hope she's gone when I get back so I don't have to deal with her."

"Haven't you spoken to her to make sure?"

"I told her during a phone call on Friday evening to make sure she was gone by Tuesday."

"Aren't you worried she might take something of yours?"

"No. The doorman is aware that nothing should leave the apartment other than her and her suitcases."

"Well, hopefully she will be gone when you get there. If you don't mind my asking, were you together long?" Kate moved the menu closer.

"A little over two years. Last week I picked up the extension to make a call and heard her on the phone with this other woman."

"Not very smart to make that call with you in the house."

"She thought I had already left, but I forgot a file and went back to grab it. That's when I heard her on the phone giggling. Of course, I got suspicious. She's on the phone giggling not even sixty seconds after I leave?" Lane opened her menu.

"What did you do?"

"I went in the kitchen and picked up the other phone. I hoped I was wrong and would owe her an apology, but that wasn't the case. I covered the receiver so they couldn't hear me and listened until I couldn't take it anymore. I went to the bedroom to confront her. You should have seen the look on her face."

"Surprise!"

"She immediately changed the topic of conversation. She didn't know I had been listening. I walked over to her, took the phone out of her hand, and hung it up."

"Tough to explain away."

"Believe me, she tried, but once I told her everything I heard, she had no choice but to come clean."

The waiter came to ask if they were ready to order. After looking over the menu and a quick discussion of the specials they continued their conversation.

"No chance of reconciliation?" Kate asked.

"Call me funny, but I think once someone cheats on you, that's it."

"Isn't that kind of harsh? Not that I'm an advocate of cheating, but aren't there sometimes extenuating circumstances?"

"To me it means that the other person is looking for something she's not finding in, or getting from me, and if it's not there, then she's going to keep looking. It just means I'm not the right person for her anymore. Plus, I would never be able to trust her again. I'd keep waiting for it to happen again, and more importantly, keep wondering what was the matter with me to make her cheat in the first place."

"My relationships have never gotten to a point of being that serious, so I haven't ever had to cross that bridge."

"Trust me, you don't want to." Lane shook her head.

The arrival of their food brought the somewhat uncomfortable conversation to a close.

"So, tell me, are you looking for a relationship?" Lane asked after a few minutes.

Kate grew a bit uncomfortable. "Lane, I really like you but—"

Lane grabbed Kate's hand. "I wasn't talking about us."

"I think we should talk about us." Kate squeezed Lane's hand gently. "I think if it's all right with you, I would like to keep seeing you and just take it slow."

"Given my current situation, the last thing I need to do is get involved with anyone. But, having said that, I really like you too and would like to see you when I come out here. Is that all right?"

Kate smiled. "Absolutely. Why don't we just take things one step at a time?"

"Yes. Let's keep things light and easy."

"I like that." Kate raised her glass. "A toast to light and easy."

"I'll drink to that."

The moonrise was spectacular as the women finished their meal. They ordered a second bottle of wine instead of dessert but left half of it behind.

***

Kate held Lane's hand on the drive home.

"Come on, I want to show you something," Lane said as she got out of the car. She met Kate half way around the car and took her by the hand. Together they went down a path to a gazebo that overlooked the bay.

"I always sit out here to collect my thoughts. Sitting here grounds me, even when it's raining." Lane patted the seat for Kate to sit next to her.

"What a beautiful night." Kate looked up at the moon. "The moon is so comforting for me."

"Really?"

"Really. I feel like I get rejuvenated by the moon beams."

"That's a pretty cool thought."

"It works for me, and of course kissing in the moonlight always helps too." Kate moved closer to Lane.

"How does that work?"

"I'll show you."

Kate took Lane in her arms and kissed her. She leaned back and looked at Lane's face. Her eyes were still closed and her mouth was slightly open.

"God, you're beautiful." Kate kissed her again, longer this time.

"I see what you mean about kissing in the moonlight." Lane sighed. They turned and looked at the moon.

Kate stood up and took Lane by the hand. They strolled back to the car fingers entwined.

"When will you be back?" Kate asked.

"Probably not for another two weeks."

"Please call me when you get home and let me know that you're all right. I really do hope you don't have a confrontation to deal with when you get there."

"I will, and me too. Thanks."

Lane walked Kate to the front door. They kissed again. It wasn't until Lane closed the door behind her that Kate turned to walk back to her car. *I could fall in love with her.*

Chapter Seventeen

KATE WAS SO ENGROSSED in her magazine she didn't hear the office door open. Someone clearing their throat got her attention. When she looked up, she found a stern looking older woman staring at her.

"May I help you?" *Could this be a new client? Hopefully she's not looking for the store that was here last year.*

"If you're Kate Whitfield, then yes."

"Yes, ma'am, I am Kate Whitfield. How may I help you?" Kate came around her desk and offered her hand. The woman responded with a firm handshake.

"I'm Marjorie Winters. I've been told by some of my friends that you might be able to help me with a situation I'm having."

"Please, sit down." Kate motioned to the chair in front of her desk. "Let's see how I might be of help." Kate's mind was racing. *Can this be something? I know this name, Winters. The Winters family has been on the island for generations.*

"Can I get you anything? Water, coffee, tea?" she asked.

"No thank you dear. I'm just fine."

Kate sat down and grabbed a pen and paper.

"I'm here because my son is trying to take over my finances and put me out of my house. I'm not about to let him do that." Ms. Winters placed her purse in her lap.

"What makes him think he can?"

"Well, he has it in his head that I'm old and shouldn't be living in such a big house by myself, and that I have no idea how to manage my money."

"Are you having any issues with your health that might make him think that you're incapable of physically taking care of yourself?" Kate started making notes.

"No. It's more like he has a girlfriend who wants money that he doesn't have. So, in order for him to get some, he's trying to make me look incompetent."

"What about your assets? Are they protected? Do you have an attorney or financial advisor who handles your income and assets?"

"Well, I did, but he passed away recently. That's why my son, Randolph, is making this move on me now."

"What is it you'd like me to do?"

Marjorie looked Kate in the eye.

"Stop him in his tracks and send him running."

"I like your style, Mrs. Winters." Kate grinned.

"Oh no, dear, it's Ms. Winters, and please call me Marjorie. I never went by my married name. My family name is something to be proud of."

"Ah, yes. Your family was one of the first families on the island. You live in the Wintergarden mansion on the hill just out of town, right?"

"That's me." Marjorie smiled at Kate. "My brother and I are the only ones left now other than the children and grandchildren. Some of them will carry on here long after we are gone. Except for Randolph. He has never had any interest in this island or our family, so I'm sure as hell not about to let him come here now and cause trouble. I have helped over the years to make sure he didn't end up in the street, and I've provided for him in my will, but nothing like he thinks he deserves or is trying to get."

Kate felt the adrenalin pumping through her body. She lived for this kind of shit. "Okay, Marjorie, the first thing you are going to have to do is provide me with a copy of your will and all your financials so that I can see what you have and how best to protect you and your assets."

"I can have that to you by this afternoon. When my attorney died, his administrative staff forwarded me all my files. I will also call my banker and have him call you so that you can get any additional information you may need."

Kate was overwhelmed. "So, you want me to be your new attorney?"

"Why, yes, dear, and of course there is the matter of your fee." Marjorie reached into her purse and pulled out a check.

"This should cover your time to start." She handed Kate the check, which was already made out to her.

"Uh, Marjorie, this is for ten thousand dollars."

"Oh my, is that not enough?"

"No, no. This is more than enough. In fact, it's too much. I haven't done anything yet." *I've got to set a retainer fee.*

Marjorie stood up. "Well then, why don't we just use this as a starting balance? As you do the work and need more, we'll go from there."

Kate collected herself and stood up. "I, I...we can do that. Sure."

"Good." Marjorie took a card out of her purse and handed it to Kate. "This has all my information on it. Call me for anything you need." She turned to leave.

"Marjorie," Kate called to her, "may I ask who referred you?"

Marjorie smiled. "I think that will come out in due time."

Kate watched as Marjorie closed the door and disappeared. She sat down and looked at the check. *What just happened here?* She started laughing. *Well, I guess I just got my first client.*

Later that afternoon, boxes of Marjorie's files were delivered to the office, and her bank called to let Kate know that a bank officer had been assigned to help her with anything she needed for the case.

***

Constance was in the kitchen cutting up vegetables for dinner when Kate arrived home. "Hello, dear. Did you have a good day?"

Kate kissed her aunt on the cheek. "The best. You're not going to believe this." Kate grabbed a carrot. "I have my first client." She danced around waving the carrot.

Constance put her knife down and turned to face Kate. "Why, that's wonderful. Who is it? Or am I not allowed to ask?"

"I can tell you, but I can't tell you any specifics."

"No, of course not."

"It's Marjorie Winters." Kate took a bite of the carrot.

"Marjorie. Really?"

"Do you know her, Aunt Connie? I mean, I guess you know just about everyone on the island."

"Yes. I've known Marjorie for years. You know, bridge clubs, garden clubs...in the same circles but not in each other's inner circles." Constance nodded.

"You are now looking at her new attorney, and I have a retainer. Oh, my god, I need to have her sign a contract. I'm used to having an assistant to do the start-up work."

"Congratulations, dear. This is a great way for you to get back in the swing of things. Get in there, roll your sleeves up, and take care of business."

"I know. Some of her files have already been delivered. I think this case will be interesting."

"Well, I'm just delighted for you, dear. Why don't we celebrate with a bottle of champagne?" Constance touched Kate's arm.

"Sounds great to me."

Constance pulled a bottle from the refrigerator. "Why don't you open this while I tend to everything on the stove?"

Kate noticed all the pots simmering on the stove. "Wow, Aunt Connie, is all this for dinner?"

Constance stirred one of the pots. "Some is for dinner. The rest is for lunch tomorrow. You remember that Richard Brodman is coming?"

Between meeting Lane and getting her first client, Kate had forgotten, but she wouldn't let her aunt know that. "Of course. Twelve-thirty. I'll be here. Do you need any help? I can help you tonight or I can come home early tomorrow."

"That's quite all right, dear. I have just about everything ready, and of course, Patsy will be here early in the morning to help me."

Kate poured the champagne and handed a glass to Constance. "Thank you, Aunt Connie."

Constance looked puzzled. "For what, dear? I haven't done anything."

"Really?" Kate laughed. "Okay, let's start with you letting me stay here. And then you give me cars. You rent me office space. And I'm sure there's more I'm not thinking of."

"My dear, we all find our own luck. Sometimes it happens with a little help from others, but in the end, your life is what you make it." Constance touched Kate's glass with hers. "Always aim for the stars."

That's something Gran would have said. Kate wiped a tear from the corner of her eye. Later that night, as she pulled the blankets around her, Kate looked out the window at the twinkling stars. Aim for the stars. *Aim for the stars. Aim for the stars,* she thought as she drifted off to sleep.

Chapter Eighteen

EAGER TO GET STARTED, Kate was up and in the office early the next morning. She promised her aunt she'd be at the house by eleven forty-five to help with any last-minute tasks Constance and Patsy couldn't handle. She was familiarizing herself with Marjorie's files when her phone rang.

"Miss me?"

It took Kate a second to process the voice. "Faith, how are you?"

"Lonely."

"I'm sure that's one thing you never are." Kate stared out the window at the Mercedes parked in front of the office.

"Well, I'm lonely for you. Why don't you come have lunch with me?"

"While that is ever so appealing, I have a business lunch today."

"Really?"

"Yes, really, but what about tomorrow or Friday? Or why don't you come out here Saturday?"

"I have some charity engagements over the next few days, so I guess I'll just have to call you."

"Okay, but make it soon." Kate thought she could use a little entertainment.

"I sure will."

"Bye, Faith."

Before Kate knew it, it was eleven-thirty. She drove home with the top down, thinking about her grandmother. Sometimes she could almost feel her grandmother hugging her. It was a feeling she cherished.

After she parked the Mercedes in the garage, she went into the house through the mudroom. She heard laughter coming from the kitchen. Constance and Patsy were putting the finishing touches on lunch.

"Hi there, kiddo," Patsy said as she removed her apron.

"There you are, dear. Just in time." Constance was taking a dish from the refrigerator.

"How can I help?" Kate asked.

Constance stacked plates on the counter and removed her apron. "We are all set. When Richard arrives, we will go to the patio for iced tea and lemonade. After we talk and take care of business, we will serve lunch."

"I hope that Dex comes," Kate said.

Constance and Patsy had barely sat down when a car pulled in the driveway. "That will be Richard." Constance left the kitchen and returned a minute later followed by a handsome gentleman about seventy-five years old. He was well-dressed, tall and thin with thick white hair and a big smile.

"Good afternoon, ladies," he said as they entered the kitchen.

"Hello, Richard." Patsy stood up and kissed him on the cheek.

"Richard, I'd like you to meet my granddaughter, Kate," Constance said.

Kate extended her hand. "It's nice to meet you."

He took her hand and kissed it. "Why, the pleasure is all mine."

"And I believe," Constance continued, "that you know Dex."

Dex followed his father into the kitchen. "Hello, all."

"Dex! You did come." Kate threw her arms around his neck. "Oh, it's so good to see you again."

"You too." Dex returned Kate's hug.

"Let's move out to the patio." Constance gestured to the door. Kate and Patsy followed with food and plates.

"Do have you any clients yet?" Dex asked as he poured himself some iced tea.

"I signed my first client last week," Kate said.

"It just takes one to get things started." Richard smiled at her.

"I hope this will be the beginning of a practice that will give me the chance to really be of value to my clients." Kate placed her napkin on her lap.

Richard shared how he got started, first working as an assistant district attorney in Manhattan before joining a private practice and then forming his own firm. "And now it gives me great pleasure to be working alongside my son."

"And I have the great pleasure of learning from the person I admire most." Dex raised his glass to his father.

Casual conversation continued while everyone enjoyed Constance's sandwiches and salad. When everyone finished eating, Kate and Dex cleared the table.

"So," Dex said, "are things really going well?"

"Yes. I'm still not sure where this is heading but at least I feel alive again."

"Will you stay here or move into your own house?"

"I haven't thought about that. I mean, this house is big enough for both me and Aunt Connie."

"Your aunt is okay with you being here?"

"What do you mean?" Kate leaned against the counter and studied Dex's face.

"She has a life too. Don't you think she believes you're staying here only until you get on your feet?"

"We haven't talked about the future. I've just been taking it a day at a time."

"Well, I suppose you can figure it out as you go along, but what if you meet someone?"

Kate thought of Faith and Lane. "If that should happen, for the time being I'll have to make other arrangements."

Dex smiled. "So, you've met someone?"

"I have some interests." Kate grinned at him.

"Do tell." He waggled his eyebrows at her.

"No. I don't kiss and tell."

"Come on. It's not like I'm going to know who it is."

Kate threw a towel at him. "For right now, that's the way it's going to stay. Come on, let's get back out there."

"Oh, good. You're back. I want you both to hear this," Constance said when they rejoined the others. She turned back to Richard. "Now you know, Richard, I'm counting on you again this year to emcee our fundraiser for the historical society."

"Of course. I'll be happy to."

"Dex, it would be wonderful if you and your wife could make it this year."

Dex looked at Kate. "I think that can be arranged. I'm sure my dad can fill me in on the date and time."

"He can, but we'll send out formal invitations. I hope, Kate, that you'll be on board to help out."

"Of course. I'm sure there's something I can do."

"It's always a hoot, kiddo. You'll have a great time." Patsy winked at her. Kate knew when Patsy winked it meant a good time.

"Well, I hate to leave, but I think Dex and I should head back to the office." Richard pushed himself away from the table. "We certainly have enjoyed your delicious lunch, Constance, as well as the pleasant company of you lovely ladies."

"As always, it's been a pleasure to see you, Richard. And Dex, it was wonderful to meet you." Constance stood up.

"Wonderful to meet you as well." Dex shook Constance's hand and then Patsy's.

"I'll walk you to your car," Kate said as she linked her arm in Dex's.

"Call me and let me know how you're doing, okay? Or come have lunch with me." Dex kissed Kate on the cheek.

"I will. Keep your fingers crossed for me. Take care, Richard." Kate waved good-bye and headed back to the patio.

"That was lovely, Aunt Connie," she said as she sat in the chair beside her aunt.

"Thank you, dear. It's always good to see Richard, and I feel that speaking over the phone is just too impersonal."

"I think it's nice to have some good-looking men around for a change." Patsy sipped her lemonade.

Kate looked at her watch. "If you ladies don't need me anymore, I'll go back to the office."

"That's fine, dear. Patsy and I will just sit and enjoy this beautiful day for a little longer."

"Yes, but only after I get something to spice up this lemonade. Come on, Kate. I'll walk you up the path." Patsy held out her hand, and Kate pulled her up from the chair.

"Patsy, can I ask you something?" Kate asked as they walked arm in arm.

"Sure, kid, what is it?"

"Dex asked me today about my future plans and if Aunt Connie was wondering how long I'm going to stay here. You think it's okay I'm here with no real plans to move on, or should I be making other arrangements?"

Patsy sighed and glanced back at Constance.

"You're just fine here. Your aunt loves having you here and is very happy that she can help you."

"Really, Patsy? That sounded a little rehearsed." Kate turned and looked Patsy in the eye.

"No, really. Everything is fine. You have nothing to be concerned about. Now scoot on back to the office."

Chapter Nineteen

KATE COULDN'T HELP HERSELF any longer and by Friday afternoon she called Faith and convinced her to get a room off island for Saturday night. She told her aunt she was going to a party with Natalie and would spend the night on the mainland. Kate and Faith met for dinner at a quiet restaurant before going to the hotel where they enjoyed each other for dessert. They slept soundly in each other's arms until morning. Faith emerged from the bathroom wrapped in a plush burgundy robe, her hair still dripping, just as Kate rolled the room service cart to the dinette table near the window.

"Thank God. I'm starving," Faith said, tightening her robe. She sat down and began lifting lids. Kate watched Faith as she looked at the food.

Kate smiled as she sat down. "I could have taken you out for brunch, you know."

"Yes, I know. But this is so much more relaxing."

"You afraid someone might see us?" Kate took a plate and handed one to Faith.

"Not at all. People see me out all the time. They don't know what I'm doing, and if they do, screw them, they can't affect my life." Faith reached for the coffee pot.

"Is the only person that could affect your life your husband?"

"We have an understanding, and as long as neither one of us breaches the boundaries of that understanding, we're fine."

"What happens if you meet someone that you want to be with?" Kate took the teapot and poured some tea in her cup.

"You mean like fall in love with someone?"

"Yes."

"Well, that would be an issue because they'd have to provide me with everything I already have. I'm not about to give all this up to start over."

"But what about your own interests? Like having a career."

"Oh, please. A career?" Faith sipped her coffee.

"Seriously, Faith. Haven't you ever thought about taking care of yourself and not living with someone you have an 'understanding' with?" Kate highlighted the word 'understanding' with air quotes.

"No, why would I?"

"I don't know. Self-respect, maybe?"

"I have plenty of self-respect, and believe me, people respect me."

Kate could see Faith was getting annoyed by the direction the conversation was going. "I just meant that you're probably very talented, and I'd hate to see you miss out on anything. But if you're happy, that's all that matters." Kate got up and kissed her and then returned to her breakfast. She hadn't realized how hungry she was.

"Interior decorator," Faith said.

"I'm sorry? What?"

"I studied interior design in college and wanted to be an interior decorator. All my friends ask me for help when they're remodeling or redecorating."

"See? That's what I mean. You have an interest, and if you wanted to, I bet you could build a business and be able to take care of yourself and do what you want."

Faith was quiet for a moment. "Do you think you would be more interested in me if I were in that position now?"

Kate thought about that for a moment. "I always look for the potential in people. As far as you and I go, our situation is pretty clear. You're married, and the type of relationship that we have is all it can be."

"All it can be, as in?"

"As in, an affair."

"Oh." Faith finished her coffee and poured herself more.

"You've told me you have an open relationship with your husband, so don't you essentially have affairs?"

"I have relationships."

"What does that mean?" Kate gave her a puzzled look.

"It means I usually have meaningful relationships with women and keep most of them as friends after the relationship ends for whatever reason."

"Friends with benefits, or do they become friends when the affair is over?"

"What are you trying to get at?" Faith's expression turned angry.

"I'm trying to understand where we are going. I mean, it's obvious that it wouldn't be in my best interests to develop any deep feelings for you. When our affair is over, for whatever reason, we'll just be friends."

Faith lifted a glass of orange juice to her lips but set it down without taking a sip. "Are you starting to have feelings for me?"

Kate hadn't realized how far the conversation had gone. She hesitated a moment before answering. "I care. I care for you, otherwise I wouldn't be here. I'm not the kind of girl who has affairs. I mean, up until my world got turned upside down, I didn't have time for anything except work."

Faith's eyes welled up. "I don't know what to say."

Kate knelt next to Faith. "Look, Faith. I'm not putting any pressure on you, and I don't want any pressure on me either. I think what we have is working quite nicely."

Faith collected herself. "So do I. Hey, the food's getting cold."

Kate took her hand. "Faith."

"Let's not make any more of a big deal of this than it needs to be."

"Okay."

Kate returned to her seat. She wanted to say more but didn't. They chatted about nothing in particular, and when they were done eating, Faith got dressed and gathered her things.

"Are you sure you don't want to hang out a little longer?" Kate asked.

Faith walked to the door. "I have to go."

Kate followed her and Faith gave Kate a long, slow kiss. She pulled away, slipped on her sunglasses, and was gone.

Kate waited a moment before closing the door behind her.

Chapter Twenty

"SO, DID WE HAVE a fun evening?" Natalie came to Kate's office Monday morning to get the scoop.

"Yes, we did." Kate smiled, not wanting to tell any other details.

"Were you with Lane?"

"No. Lane's still in the City."

"Ah ha!" Natalie pointed at Kate with a huge grin on her face.

"Ah ha, what?"

"That means that you were with someone else. Interesting." Natalie tapped her finger on her chin.

Kate shuffled some papers. "Interesting how?"

"It means that you're juggling more than one girl. That could be dangerous."

"You are reading way too much into this. Besides, who says you can't see more than one person at a time?"

"The one who's going to get jealous or hurt."

"I think I'm okay, but thank you for your concern." Kate picked up a pen.

"Okay, if you say so. I just thought I'd stop by in case I needed to know any details about the cover story."

"Thanks again for that, Natalie. I really do appreciate it."

"You're welcome. Any time." She and her smirk headed out the door. She held the door open for someone and said, "Good morning."

The mailman had a certified letter for Kate. She signed for it and he handed it to her with a smile. "Enjoy your day."

"Thanks. You too," Kate said.

Kate wasn't surprised by the contents of the envelope. She had been proactive and had already secured all of Marjorie's accounts and holdings. Randolph had filed suit to have his mother evicted from her home and to allow him to take control of her assets.

"You think your mother's going to let this go quietly? Well, you have another think coming, you little worm. We'll see you in court." Kate responded to the suit and got the ball rolling.

Then she called Marjorie. "Hello Marjorie. It's Kate."

"Hello. How are you?"

"I'm fine. I wanted to let you know that Randolph is moving ahead with his suit."

"Why, that little scoundrel, thinking he could do this to me for some floozy." The tone of Marjorie's voice rose.

"Well, you knew it was coming. Good thing too. This way you were prepared for it."

"Thanks to you."

"I'll let you know as soon as we get a court date so that we can meet and go over all the details. You're going to need your character witnesses to be ready." Kate was leaning back in her chair when she realized she was dangerously close to falling over. She steadied herself.

"I will call them today and let them know that the little son of a bitch is taking this to court."

Kate pulled the receiver away from her ear and looked at it for a second. She hadn't expected that reaction. She chuckled.

"Okay, then. We'll talk soon."

"Bye, Kate. Thank you."

Kate's adrenaline was pumping. *Back in court. Wow, it's been a while.* She was confident she would win this case. With great satisfaction, she leaned back in her chair and folded her hands behind her head.

"And she's back." she said out loud.

Later that afternoon, Kate learned that the hearing had been scheduled for two weeks from that day. *Plenty of time,* she thought as she opened her calendar to plan her course of action. She had to prep the witnesses so they'd know what to expect, but she also needed to prepare Marjorie. Kate expected Randolph to play dirty, and she knew it could catch Marjorie off guard. If there was one thing Kate knew for sure, it was that many families had been ripped apart by greed. As Kate was looking over her notes, she was interrupted by the ringing of her phone.

"Kate Whitfield."

"Lane Bellows."

"Hey, Lane. What a lovely surprise. How are you?" Kate sat back in her chair. "Did you get my message?"

"Yes. Thanks for the call."

"I really meant what I said. Any time you want to talk, you can call me."

"I'm fine. Things went a lot smoother than I thought. Honestly, I've just been busy with patients. I wanted to call and let you know I was thinking about coming out Friday."

"That would be great." Kate moved her notes to the side of her desk.

"I hope we can get together."

Since she had spent time with Faith that weekend, Kate didn't hesitate.

"I have no plans. That is, unless Aunt Connie made some plans she hasn't told me about yet." Kate laughed.

"My grandmother loves to do that to me too. There is a potluck Friday night."

"We could go to it or do something else while they're occupied. Why don't we think about it and talk on Friday when you get here?" Kate checked her calendar to see if she had anything listed.

"Sounds like a plan. I'll catch the early train and call you when I get to the house."

"Great. Looking forward to seeing you."

"Likewise. Bye."

Kate turned her chair and stared out the window. She laughed. *Oh, I can hear Natalie now.*

Chapter Twenty-one

KATE SPENT THE WEEK poring over files and making notes. Her first foray back into the world of law was not going to end in defeat. She had dinner each night with Constance, who was eager to hear how the case was progressing. Kate told her as much as she could without breaching client confidentiality. In return, Constance offered her own insight, sometimes offering a perspective Kate hadn't considered. Kate enjoyed the quality time she spent with her aunt.

"Are you coming with us tomorrow night?" Constance asked as she loaded the dinner dishes into the dishwasher.

"I'm not sure, Aunt Connie. Lane is coming out for the weekend and I thought we might catch a movie or something." Kate closed the refrigerator and turned to face Constance

"I'm not sure if Ellie is going to be all that thrilled about that," Constance said.

"Why? What's wrong with a movie?"

"Well, dear, we will be discussing the historical society gala tomorrow night, and Ellie and Lane are on the committee. I have a feeling that if Lane is going to be in town, Ellie will want her to participate in the event planning."

"Oh. Of course. That makes sense." Kate relaxed. "Okay, when Lane calls, I'll see what she says and we'll take it from there. We can go to a movie Saturday night."

"I'm so glad you are making nice friends while you are here, dear." Constance smiled at Kate. "Excuse me, won't you? I must go call Patsy. She wants to make the same dish I plan to make, but I make it so much better than she does. I'm trying to convince her to make something else."

Kate laughed. "Good luck!"

Kate retrieved some files from her briefcase and went to the patio to do some reading while she still had some light. The days were getting warmer and Kate noticed more people out in their boats at sunset. She couldn't blame them. The colors reflecting off the water were mesmerizing. Distracted from her reading by the boats on the water, Kate watched as the night sky took over and the boats danced in the water among the twinkling stars and moonbeams.

Kate finally went back inside and said goodnight to Constance, who was still on the phone, bickering with Patsy over who should make what for the potluck. She knew Aunt Connie was going to win. Upstairs, she fell asleep as soon as her head hit the pillow.

The next morning, she came downstairs to an empty kitchen. A note next to a plate of scones read, 'Gone shopping with Patsy. See you later.' She turned on the kettle for tea and glanced at the clock. If Lane caught the early train, she would be at the other side of the ferry in about half an hour. Kate raced upstairs and got dressed. Back downstairs she poured hot water over a tea bag in a travel cup and grabbed a scone as she raced through the kitchen. It was a Mercedes kind of day and Kate enjoyed the ride through town. She couldn't stop smiling.

Kate pulled into the ferry lane and followed the ferry attendant's direction for parking on the deck near the back of the ferry. She got out of the car and made her way to the railing. The water was calm and a slight breeze brushed her cheek. She sipped her tea and finished the scone as she strained to see if the train was at the station. *Good. It's not there yet.*

When the ferry docked, she was off and pulled into the station just in time to hear the train whistle. Kate got out of the car to watch. She had always loved trains, so she wasn't surprised when she felt the excitement grow, although she did wonder how much of it was because she was about to see Lane again.

The locomotive lumbered into the quaint station pulling two passenger cars behind it. Kate walked up the ramp to the platform so she wouldn't miss Lane. When the train finally stopped, the doors opened and the passengers began to trickle off the train. Kate moved down the platform and peered into the first car. Empty. Heading toward the second car, Kate spied Lane carrying an arm load of shopping bags and an overnight case in tow behind her.

Lane's eyes opened wide as she spotted Kate. "Kate?"

"Hi." Kate started taking packages away from Lane.

"What are you doing here?"

"I came to surprise you, and by the look on your face, it was a good decision since I'm going to be able to save you from this shopping bag attack."

Lane set the bags down.

"There you are." Kate smiled as gave her a long hug.

"This is a nice surprise," Lane said, hugging her back.

When they separated, they each reached for a handful of bags.

"What's with all the bags?" Kate asked.

"Well, on my way through the train station, I spotted a few irresistible sales. It was time to buy new things for the summer and change out some stuff from last year anyway."

Kate laughed so hard Lane stopped walking to look at her. "Sorry, Lane. It's just that, for me, shopping is a necessary evil. That's not to say that now and again I don't spot something in a shop window that gets my attention, but in general, it doesn't excite me."

"Well, I love to shop, so if you ever want to go, just let me know," Lane said as they started toward the parking lot once again.

"I promise, if I ever get the urge, I'll let you know." *If nothing else, it will be a good excuse to spend more time with her.*

They loaded everything into the Mercedes and drove to the ferry. The ride back to the island was full of laughter and conversation.

"By the way, when I mentioned to Aunt Connie that you and I might be going to a movie tonight, she said your grandmother might expect you at the potluck to discuss the gala." Kate winked when she mentioned going to the movies. Lane grinned and blushed.

"My grandmother already reminded me about that. Maybe we can go the movies tomorrow night?"

"How long are you staying?" Kate asked as she pulled the car off the ferry and headed for the main road.

"Until Tuesday."

"If you don't have any plans for today, we could grab some sandwiches and drinks and take the boat out."

"I would love to. I need to change first though."

"Okay, so here's the plan. We stop in town and get some food. Then I'll drop you off so you can change your clothes. I'll run back to the house and change clothes. Then I'll come back and get you."

"Sounds good. Is the boat at the marina?" Lane asked.

"No. The Boston Whaler's in the boat house at Aunt Connie's."

"Well, then there's no sense in you coming back to get me. I'll drive over. I keep a car here on the island.

"Are you sure?"

"Absolutely. Give me a few minutes to catch up with my grandmother and I'll be on my way."

"Sounds great." Kate smiled.

After they stopped for sandwiches and drinks, Kate dropped Lane off at her grandmother's house and went home. She parked the car and bounded up the walkway, bursting through the mudroom door and into the kitchen. Just as she put her foot on the first stair, Aunt Connie called to her from the sunroom.

Kate headed for the sunroom, talking as she went. "Hey, Aunt Connie, I was just about to come and ask you if you'd mind—" Kate stopped short. "Mom!"

"There's my girl." Morgan stood to greet her daughter.

Kate ran into her arms.

"Oh, my god, Mom, it's so good to see you." Kate hugged her mother then stepped back. "How did you get here?"

"The train."

"I just came from the train." Kate looked puzzled.

"I know. I saw you and had to hide behind people to sneak by you and your friend." Morgan smiled at her. "Slipping onto the ferry was a little easier."

"That was my friend, Lane. Oh, my god. I can't believe you're here. This is a wonderful surprise. Where's Dad?" Kate hugged her mother again.

"He promised to come next time. I thought we could get some girl time to ourselves."

Kate looked at Constance. "Did you know she was coming, Aunt Connie?"

"Why, yes, dear. She called earlier in the week, but we thought it would be a nice surprise for you."

"It certainly is." Kate beamed. Although she talked to her mother regularly, it wasn't the same as being near her.

"Why don't you two sit down and I'll start working on lunch? Patsy will be here in a flash. She was so excited to hear you were coming."

"You mean Patsy knew too?" Kate asked.

"Of course, dear." Constance smiled and went to the kitchen.

"Thank you, Aunt Connie," Morgan called after her.

"So," Morgan grabbed both of Kate's hands. "Let me have a look at you."

Kate released her grip and spun around.

"No worse for wear, I see. I take it you've been getting along fine?"

"Things are going well, yes."

"And if that pretty blonde at the station is any indication, things are going much better than you thought they would." Morgan tapped her finger on Kate's nose.

"Ah, Lane." Kate couldn't contain her smile.

"Lane. That's a pretty name for a pretty girl."

Morgan sat on the sofa and patted the cushion beside her. "Sit with me."

"She's Eleanor Bellows' granddaughter." Kate sat next to Morgan.

"I remember Ellie."

"We met at an outing one day and see each other when she's here."

"She doesn't live on the island?"

"No. She's a cardiologist and lives in Manhattan. She comes out on weekends when she can."

"When do I get to meet her?"

"Oh no! I've got to call and tell her we can't go out on the boat." Kate jumped to her feet.

"You had plans to go out on the boat?"

"I just came home to change clothes and ask Aunt Connie if she minded if I took the Boston Whaler out for a little while."

"Well, don't let me stop you, dear-heart."

"But you just got here. I don't want to leave you." Kate leaned over and hugged her mother.

"Dear-heart, we have all weekend to catch up. Not to worry." Morgan kissed the top of Kate's head.

They looked up when they heard the mudroom door open and close. "All right, Morgan, where are you?" Patsy bellowed.

"In here, Pats."

Patsy appeared and Morgan ran to her for a hug.

Patsy glowed. "Having you and Kate out here? Doesn't get much better than this." She squeezed Morgan's cheeks.

"Oh, Patsy, I've missed you."

"Missed you too, kiddo. Come on, let's go find Connie and shake things up a bit." Patsy waved for Kate to join them and the three of them headed for the kitchen.

"Isn't this great, Connie?" Patsy said as she went to stand next to her friend. "Now, if we can convince Morgan to stay out until the gala, life would be wonderful."

Kate looked at her Mom. "I forgot you and Dad come out for the gala."

"I think we only missed one year and that was because we were in Spain."

There was a light knock on the mudroom door. "Hello?" Lane called out.

Kate raced to greet her. "Hey. Come in. I have a surprise." Kate guided Lane into the kitchen. "Aunt Connie, Patsy, you know Lane."

"Hello, dear," they said in unison.

"Lane, I'd like you to meet my mother, Morgan Whitfield. Mom, this is Lane Bellows."

"Nice to meet you, Lane." Morgan walked over and extended her hand.

"Oh, my gosh, it's such a pleasure to meet you, Ms. Whitfield. I'm a huge fan." Lane shook Morgan's hand.

"Please, Lane, call me Morgan."

"Mom, Lane has one of your paintings in her apartment," Kate said with a smile.

"Really, dear? How flattering."

"Yes. It's *Sunlight in the Shadows*. I won it at an art gallery auction. I almost couldn't pay my rent after outbidding another woman who also wanted it, but it was worth it. I'd love to know the story behind it."

Morgan was momentarily stunned.

Before she had a chance to answer, Constance said, "I hope you girls will stay for lunch on the patio." She had prepared a tray of sandwiches

Kate and Lane looked at each other. Lane smiled and nodded her head.

"If we are all in agreement, girls?" Morgan asked.

"Yes," Kate and Lane answered together.

"I don't think that's an offer we can pass up, Aunt Connie." Morgan smiled.

"Good. Then you can help me carry the rest of the trays."

Over the course of the afternoon, Morgan and Lane got to know each other and Constance and Patsy updated Morgan on all the island gossip, much to Kate and Lane's amusement. At one point, Kate looked around the table at the smiling, laughing faces. Three she knew she loved and one she knew she was falling in love with.

Patsy clinked her glass with her fork. "Now, ladies, let's not get too carried away this afternoon. You know we have a potluck to attend."

"Patsy's right. There will be serious matters to be discussed," Constance said.

"Well, I hate to say it, but I'd better head home and get ready. My grandmother will be tapping her foot at me if I'm not ready on time," Lane said as she stood up.

"I'm glad you stayed, Lane. It was a pleasure to meet you." Morgan got up and hugged her.

"Thank you, and thank you all for a lovely afternoon."

"I'll walk you out." Kate got up and fell in step next to Lane. They walked down the path to Lane's car.

"Thanks for taking the change in plans in stride. I know it wasn't the boat ride we talked about." Kate touched Lane's arm.

"Are you kidding? I can't believe I met *the* Morgan Whitfield. I wouldn't have passed that up for anything. And I enjoyed myself. They're all wonderful women. We can spend another day on the boat."

"So, I'll see you later?"

"You most certainly will." Lane leaned in and kissed Kate gently on the lips before climbing in the car and driving up the driveway.

Kate smiled as she watched her go and then went back to the patio.

"She's lovely, dear-heart," Morgan said when Kate rejoined the group.

"Isn't she?" Kate sat down and grabbed her mother's hand.

Chapter Twenty-two

NOT SURPRISINGLY, THE MAIN discussion at the evening's potluck quickly shifted from the historical society's gala to the latest details of Morgan's life. Kate watched with amusement as her mother held court and shared stories of her latest endeavors in the art world.

Lane sat down next to Kate with a plate of food. "Your mother is wonderful."

Kate smiled. "She sure is."

"She's beautiful, artistic, and so nice."

"I can't argue with you." Kate snuck a shrimp off Lane's plate and popped it into her mouth.

"Hey!" Lane scolded her.

"I thought we were sharing." Kate gave her an innocent smile.

"Okay, I'll share."

Kate grabbed another shrimp.

"But," Lane said. "You have to refill the plate when we're done."

"Deal."

"I was talking to your mother while I was filling our plate. I think I could just talk to her for hours."

"Maybe we can have dinner or brunch or lunch with her before you both leave."

"That would be so cool." Lane nodded.

"What would be even better would be if we could have some alone time."

"I agree, but since your mother is here, I think we'll just have to see what happens."

"If nothing else, we need to hit the beach or take the boat out. We bought all that food today." Kate took another shrimp.

Lane laughed. "Try the crab cakes."

***

The next morning, when Kate came downstairs, she saw Constance and Morgan deep in conversation at the table on the patio. *Man, if that table could talk*, she thought as she poured some tea, grabbed her mug, and joined them.

"Good morning, my girl. How are you this morning?" Morgan asked, smiling up at Kate.

"Morning, Mom. Morning, Aunt Connie." Kate kissed her mother on the cheek and sat down in the seat next to her. "I'm fine. How are you?"

"Wonderful. I always sleep like a baby when I'm here," Morgan said.

"Your mother and I were just discussing the day, dear." Constance passed a plate of scones to Kate.

"Oh, yum. Orange." Kate smiled with delight as she took one.

"So, Mom?" Kate said as she took a bite of her scone, realizing too late the blunder she'd made. *Uh oh, chew first. No sense in starting the day with a disapproving look from Aunt Connie.* Kate finished chewing and swallowed. "We didn't get to talk much last night. How long are you staying?"

Morgan and Constance exchanged glances.

"What's going on?" Kate asked.

"Well, dear-heart, I haven't decided. I thought about staying until the gala and doing some painting while I'm here. I'm always so inspired by this place. But I'm also thinking I might go home and come back with your father a few days before the gala. I'll just see how the weekend goes. Don't you and Lane have plans?"

"We were going to go out on the Whaler." Kate sipped her tea.

"What do you mean, 'were?' Aren't you going to go do that?" Morgan asked.

"No. I don't want to leave you."

"How about if I come along? I'd like to go over to the cove. I have a painting in mind."

"I'll call Lane. I'm sure she'll be fine with that." Kate got up from the table.

"Great, but tonight, you and Lane go have some fun together. I'm sure Aunt Connie and I can find something amusing to do."

"Of course, we can. There are a number of things we can do." Constance nodded.

It wasn't long before Kate, Lane, and Morgan were crossing the small bay and heading into the cove. They anchored the boat and waded through the clear, warm water to the beach. Kate and Lane set up the chairs and umbrella while Morgan took her paint box and chair to find the perfect spot to paint. Kate looked out over the tranquil water and couldn't help but feel relaxed.

"You look so peaceful." Lane smiled at her.

"I don't know what it is about this place, but it always heals my heart and soul."

"That must be a wonderful feeling. I should prescribe it to all my patients—find something or someplace that heals your heart and soul. But then they wouldn't need me." Lane shook her head.

"It must be hard for you sometimes. I assume not everyone who comes to see you has a good outcome. I mean, you're a cardiologist. Doesn't that mean someone who comes to see you has some sort of a heart problem?" Kate moved her feet back and forth burying, them in the soft sand.

"Yes. Sometimes an issue can be resolved easily, like by getting someone's blood pressure under control." Lane paused for a minute. "But a lot of times I have to tell someone that their heart isn't functioning the way it should and then try to find a solution for them."

"Wow." Kate's eyes widened at the thought.

"But that's why I'm a doctor, to help people. And I've always been good at dealing with stressful situations while keeping my head and heart together."

"I guess that's why certain people get a calling to do a particular job." Kate picked up a small handful of sand.

"Don't you feel that way?"

"What do you mean?" Kate let the sand run out between her fingers.

"Well, not everyone could be a lawyer. I mean, how can you defend someone you know is guilty?"

"Ah, the age-old question. That's why I didn't go into criminal law. I wouldn't be able to defend someone when all the circumstances point to their guilt. I know that everyone deserves a fair trial, and that you're innocent until proven guilty, but sometimes it's pretty clear-cut that the person is guilty. In some of those cases, you can get a plea bargain, and I just couldn't stomach it."

"So, you chose corporate law?"

"It seemed the most interesting to me and it certainly was until we had a criminal in our midst." Kate shivered at the memory.

Lane leaned over and placed a soft kiss on Kate's cheek.

"I think you're going to be just fine."

Kate turned to kiss Lane. After a few moments, they pulled apart.

"Too bad my mother's nearby. I have a nice little secluded dune I'd like to show you." Kate tugged at the top of Lane's bathing suit.

"I think we need to plan some alone time before I leave." Lane stood up and reached for Kate's hand. "But for now, how about we settle for a swim?"

Kate grabbed her hand and Lane pulled her up. They ran for the water, sand flying behind them. After floating around for a while as the waves gently rocked them, they returned to the beach. Moments later, Morgan rejoined them.

"Hey there, you two, enjoying the day?" Morgan called from the sand dune.

"It's been great, Mom. How's the painting coming?" Kate went to meet her mother. She took her chair and set it up next to her own.

"Wonderful," Morgan said as she sat down.

"I'm so impressed by your talent, Morgan." Lane turned her chair more to face Morgan's.

"Why, thank you, Lane, but my talent certainly can't be compared to yours, saving people's lives and all. Now that's impressive"

"Thank you, but I really don't think I'm saving people's lives. I mean, I think the real heroes are the surgeons and the researchers, people who really make a difference." Lane shook her head.

"You're quite right about those people, but you also save lives by diagnosing and treating people. How did you decide to become a doctor?" Morgan asked.

"Oh, you don't want to hear that." Lane blushed.

"Come on, Lane. I'd like to hear it too," Kate said.

"All right." Lane took a deep breath. "When I was little, I was always helping sick and injured animals. I knew my grandmother was a doctor, but I never saw her in action, so I guess it was just a natural thing for me. My family always thought I would be a veterinarian. Then, as I got older and started coming out to the island for the summers, I got to know some of my grandmother's friends. There were two women who were always part of the group. I thought they were sisters or something. One day, my parents came to visit and my father was in the kitchen talking to my mother. I overheard him saying to my mother, 'I don't need to be around those two dykes. I can't believe your mother would even have them in her house.'"

"Really, dear? Your father?" Morgan said.

"Mom! Please. Sorry, Lane. Go on."

"My mother told him to leave if he was uncomfortable, which he did. Soon after the party started, one of the two ladies became ill. My grandmother rushed to her side and started doing CPR. All the while, the other lady sat next to her crying and saying, 'I love you, don't leave me.' Even while they were wheeling her to the ambulance, the other lady stayed with her telling her she loved her and not to leave her."

"What happened?" Kate asked when Lane paused.

"Thanks to my grandmother, she was okay. A few weeks later they both came over to thank her. It dawned on me that they were a couple like my parents. The only difference was that they really loved each other, unlike my parents. I decided then that I wanted to be a doctor so people wouldn't lose the ones they loved."

"See, dear, you are a life saver." Morgan put her arm around Lane.

"How did your father react when he found out you were gay?" Kate asked.

"I hid the fact for a long time, but when I told him, he didn't take it well at all. We barely spoke. I used to sit outside in the shadows and stare at the patches of nearby sun. I always thought that one day I would be able to walk out of the shadows into the sun and live my life."

"And so," Morgan whispered, "Sunlight in the Shadows." She opened her arms to Lane, who fell into them, crying.

It took Kate a moment or two before she made the connection. Morgan, ever the mother, dabbed Lane's tears with a tissue she had pulled out of nowhere.

"There, there. It's all right. I know it must still be difficult at times. Take a deep breath and sit up. I'll tell you the story behind the painting. When I was in college, I had a large circle of friends, but there were four of us who were very close. It was me, Carol, Celeste, and Hope. We had adjoining suites. We wore each other's clothes, shared all our secrets, and did all the other things best friends do.

"During our last year of college, Celeste became withdrawn and moody, not herself at all. She had always been carefree and outgoing, willing to take a chance on anything. None of us could figure out what was going on. When she first started to change, we blamed it on PMS and hormones, but it became really disturbing. We couldn't get her to tell us what was wrong. One night, Carol, Hope, and I went to a party without her. She said she didn't feel up to it.

"When we came back," Kate could see her mother tensing as the expression on her face changed, "She was in bed, motionless. We tried talking to her and shaking her, but she didn't move. When Carol tried to get her to sit up, a bottle of pills fell on the floor. We knew then she was in real trouble. Hope ran to get our building monitor and I called the ambulance. Carol held Celeste until the paramedics transferred her to the gurney. She died at the hospital later that night."

"Oh Mom, that's horrible." Kate said as she wiped away tears.

"Yes, it was. And what was even more horrible was why it happened." Morgan wiped away a tear. "As it turned out, Celeste had fallen in love with another girl. They were having a relationship and apparently one of the girl's friends found out and was starting rumors and saying nasty things. So much so that the girl ended the relationship. That's what started Celeste on her descent."

"But you were all so close, why didn't she tell any of you? And how did you find out?" Lane was crying again.

"She left us notes. One to me, Carol, and Hope, and another one to her parents. She said that even though she knew we would still love her and accept her, and that her parents would have felt and done the same, she herself couldn't accept the fact that she was a lesbian and she couldn't live like that. She said she would never see the sunlight through the shadows."

Kate shook her head. "I can't imagine what she must have gone through. I'm so sorry, Mom."

"It took us months to deal with it. Even after we graduated, when we'd meet, we'd still try to figure out what we could have done to help. We finally realized there probably wasn't anything we could have done. Soon after that, I was doing an outdoor landscape and something made me turn around and I caught sight through the trees of the sun and the shadows playing a game with each other. Kind of like which one was going to be the strongest. I thought of Celeste's note and what she had said and I started painting."

"But the painting," Lane choked on her words, "the painting has a feeling of such hope."

"Well, my dear, that was the point. I wanted whoever ended up with it to see the sunlight through the shadows and feel hope in their lives that nothing would ever be too much for them to overcome."

"Wow." Kate looked at Lane. "I wonder who had it before you did."

"I know the answer to that," Morgan said. "When I finished the painting, I had a small show in Manhattan. There was a gentleman there who stood in front of it all night. As the gallery was closing, he approached me and said he would like to purchase it. He thought it would give some hope to a friend who was struggling with an illness. A few years ago, I was contacted by a gallery in Manhattan and informed that the owner had brought it in to sell it because he was downsizing. They wanted to know if I knew of anyone who was interested in it. I said no but asked if they would please call me when it sold. A few months later, the gallery called to tell me they had sold the painting at an auction to a young woman who was a regular visitor to the gallery. They told me she had to battle it out with another woman to win the bid."

"I had to have it," Lane said through her tears.

"And you do." Morgan hugged her. "And I hope that it has given you all that you need."

"It's my most valued possession. I will never part with it."

"This is unbelievable." Kate went over and wrapped her arms around Morgan and Lane. They sat in silence for a while before packing up and going home.

The weekend went by in a flash. Kate and Lane took Morgan to dinner Saturday night. While they were eating, Morgan decided to leave the island and come back before the gala. Sunday morning, Kate and Lane had brunch with Patsy and Morgan. Constance and Lane's grandmother were invited to join them, but they both had other engagements. Short of a little make out time in the car when Kate took Lane home each night, they didn't have any alone time. They promised each other they would make time during Lane's next visit.

Chapter Twenty-three

KATE DROVE MARJORIE TO the courthouse the day her case was scheduled to be heard. Once inside the hearing room, Kate notified the court officer of their presence, and then she and Marjorie sat at the counsel's table. Kate pulled Marjorie's folder from her briefcase and arranged the necessary documents in front of her.

A few minutes later, the courtroom door opened and the sound of footsteps filled the room. As Kate suspected, it was Marjorie's son Randolph and his attorney. They took their places at the table across the aisle. Kate got up and introduced herself to them and returned to her seat.

"I should just go over there and hit him with my shoe," Marjorie mumbled under her breath.

"Now, now," Kate said while trying to stifle a chuckle. "Let's win the case first, then you can hit him with your shoe." Kate turned when she heard more people enter the courtroom. Patsy was accompanied by a slew of woman who filed into the back rows. Kate only recognized half of them. She looked at Marjorie.

"What the heck?"

"It's all right, dear. They're here for moral support." Marjorie smiled and waved.

"Great." Kate put her head in her hands. She had asked a few of the women to come as character witnesses in case Randolph's lawyer decided to play dirty, but she hadn't expected the full ensemble. A few more minutes passed before a second court officer and the court reporter came in. Seconds later the judge was announced and the people in the room stood up.

"Court is now in session," announced the court clerk. "The honorable Judge James Hogan presiding."

"Be seated," the judge said as he took his seat behind the bench.

The judge looked up from the paper on his desk and announced the case. "Ladies and gentlemen, this is a guardianship hearing in the case of Randolph Peterson versus Marjorie Winters for control of Ms. Winters's estate and her own well-being. Are all involved parties present?"

"Yes, your honor," the court clerk answered.

"All right, let's proceed. As I understand this, Ms. Winters is filing a counter motion to have Randolph Peterson blocked in this action and to remove him from any and all aspects of her estate now and in the future. Who is representing Ms. Winters?"

Kate stood up. "I am your honor. Katherine Whitfield."

"Thank you, Ms. Whitfield. And who is representing Mr. Peterson?"

"I am your honor. Harold Simon."

"Thank you, Mr. Simon." The judge made some notations and then began again. "All right, Mr. Simon, please present your case."

"Yes, your honor. Thank you." Mr. Simon walked around and stood in front of the table. "It is our intention to show that it is in the best interest of Marjorie Winters that her son be named as trustee of her estate in order to care for her and her interests, as she has become increasingly unable to handle these tasks in recent months."

Groans erupted from the gallery.

The judge cleared his throat and reprimanded the women. "Ladies."

"It is my client's intention to make sure that his mother is taken care of during the final years of her life. In order to do so, it is essential that she does not squander her estate so that it is available to care for her."

"Are you going to provide the court with any proof of Ms. Winters's incapacity in this matter?" the judge asked.

"Yes, your honor. Documents will show that Ms. Winters removed her son from her will and other real estate and investment holdings which he had long looked after."

"Mr. Simon, Ms. Winters has the right to include or exclude whomever she pleases from the benefits of her will and the maintaining of her investments.

"Your honor, Mr. Peterson feels that he is the best person to handle his mother's estate."

The judge put his hand up. "I'm going to stop you right there, Mr. Simon. Do you have any examples, witnesses, anything to prove that Ms. Winters is incompetent?"

"Your honor, my client would like a chance to give his opinion of his mother."

"Mr. Simon, I am not in the habit of listening to opinions without facts. Ms. Whitfield, before you present your case, would you have any objection to having your client take the stand and tell her side of this?"

Kate stood up. "May I have a moment with my client?"

"Certainly," the judge said as he nodded.

Kate sat down and leaned over to Marjorie. "Okay, Marjorie, I'm just going to ask you some simple questions about Randolph and what it is you want to do with your estate. Answer the questions the best you can and we should get this settled."

"All right, deary. Let's go." Marjorie was up and out of her chair.

Once Marjorie was sworn it and settled on the stand, Kate approached her. "As you know, Ms. Winters, we are here today to settle the matter of your estate and how and by whom you want it handled."

"Yes. I understand."

"Is it your intention that your son Randolph be the trustee of your estate?"

"No, I don't want Randolph to be able to touch a thing nor do I want him to get anything from my estate other than what I've stipulated in my will."

The gallery applauded. The judge scolded them again. "Ladies, please."

"So, you have made some provisions for your son in your will?"

"Yes, but if he tries anything else, he won't get that." Marjorie shook her finger at her son. "I have taken care of him all his life, and now, because he's got some floozy he's trying to impress, he wants it all. I've had an attorney and financial advisor handle my affairs for years, both of whom I met with monthly, and I am fully aware of what goes on. There is no reason for Randolph to be in control of anything."

Kate picked up some paperwork off the table. "Your honor, I have signed documents from Ms. Winters's financial advisor and from her previous attorney's office that these meetings did take place and that Ms. Winters was, and is, in full control of her estate. We also have taken the liberty of having Ms. Winters evaluated by a local psychologist who specializes in seniors. He has provided a report on her competency." Kate handed the reports to the clerk who handed them to the judge.

"I also have a copy of Ms. Winters's will, along with all the documents needed to be filed with it, that state that Randolph Peterson has been provided for in the will and that any attempt by him, or anyone representing him, will result in his being denied what has been provided for him." Again, Kate handed the paperwork to the clerk who handed it to the judge.

The judge looked over the paperwork. "Ms. Whitfield, would you have any objections to me speaking privately to Ms. Winters?"

"Not at all, your honor."

"Ms. Winters, would you be agreeable to joining me in my chambers for a few minutes so I may ask you a few questions?"

"Of course, your honor."

The judge motioned to one of the court officers, who then escorted her to the judge's chambers.

"This court will adjourn for thirty minutes." The judge banged his gavel and left the bench.

Kate glanced across the aisle. Randolph was clearly annoyed with his attorney. They argued back and forth for a few minutes before Randolph slammed his hand on the table, bolted out of his chair, and stormed out of the courtroom. Out of the corner of her eye, Kate spotted the court officer returning to his post. She shuffled some paperwork on the table and poured herself a glass of water.

"So, kiddo, what do you think?" Patsy sat in a chair just behind the railing separating the gallery from the court. Kate pushed her chair back so she still faced the bench but slightly turned so she could answer Patsy.

"I don't think Randolph has a case. They haven't provided anything to show that Marjorie is incapable of handling her estate. A good attorney wouldn't have even taken his case. He's proven that he wants her money." Kate took a sip of her water.

"So, you don't think he has a peg to stand on?" Patsy asked.

Kate nearly choked on her water. "Leg to stand on? No, I don't," she said as she wiped a drop of water from her lip. Patsy winked at her and went back to her seat.

A few minutes later, Marjorie and the judge emerged from the judge's chambers. The judge motioned for one of the court officers to escort Marjorie to the table.

"All rise," the same officer announced as the judge returned to the bench.

"After speaking to Ms. Winters, I have made my decision. Mr. Simon, your case lacks any evidence to prove that Marjorie Winters is incapable of handling the day-to-day aspects of her estate or her plans for the future of her estate. Based on your failure to provide such evidence, I do so hereby dismiss this case."

Cheers rose from the gallery.

The judge banged his gavel. "Mr. Simon, it is also my intention to ensure that your client, Randolph Peterson, adheres to his mother's wishes. Therefore, the following will be enacted. One: Ms. Winters will make a provision for her son, and this will be recorded. Two: An addendum to the will has also been provided such that, should Randolph Peterson, or anyone representing him, contest the will, he will be immediately disinherited, or should he already have received his inheritance, it will be rescinded and he will pay restitution to the estate. Three: Katherine Whitfield will be named executrix of the estate and will hold all duties as such. I shall expect all paperwork to be complete and on my desk within thirty days. Court is adjourned." The judge rose and exited the courtroom.

Kate was momentarily confused. Randolph's attorney closed his briefcase and left the courtroom without a word.

"Are you all right, Kate?" Marjorie patted her arm.

"Well I was, but now I don't know. Marjorie, did you just name me as executrix of your estate?"

"Yes. Was that all right? I know we hadn't discussed it, but that nice judge, well, in talking to him, he asked who besides me was better to handle my estate. I thought about it and the only logical answer was you."

"But Marjorie, surely there must be someone? Your nieces perhaps?"

Marjorie stopped her with a wave of her hand. "You, you're the only choice. You're my attorney and friend, and I know that no one will oversee my well-being and wishes better than you."

"I don't know what to say."

"Well, you'd better say yes as I won't take no for an answer."

"Marjorie, I promise I'll take good care of you and make sure all of your wishes are followed."

"I know that, and that's why there was no other choice. I also want you to help other seniors out there who might have to face something like this. You know, this old broad still has her sense about her, but others don't, and this type of thing with family can get pretty ugly."

"You mean be a senior advocate?"

"Well, dear, I don't know what your legal term might be, but I think you can count on a lot of people coming your way once they find out what you did for me."

"Thank you, Marjorie. You've given me a lot to think about." Kate smiled and grabbed her hand as Patsy and her entourage converged on Kate and Marjorie.

"Congratulations, kiddo. You did good." Patsy reached over the railing and gave Kate a hug. "Let's get the hell out of here. It reminds me too much of a TV crime show. We've got a big lunch planned at the Rose and Thistle, and I think we could all use a drink."

"Go on, ladies. I'll be right behind you."

Kate sat down and looked around the courtroom. People were starting to file in for other cases. *Wow*, she thought as she got up and picked up her briefcase, *maybe I am going to be all right after all.*

Chapter Twenty-four

KATE'S PHONE RANG LIKE crazy over the next few days. Word of Kate's win for Marjorie brought issues to the forefront for many people on the island. She was booked for the next two weeks. The phone rang again.

"Kate Whitfield."

"Seems like you've forgotten about me."

Kate flushed with mixed emotions. "Faith. How are you?"

"Fine." Never a good answer from a woman.

"I'm sorry, Faith, I've been crazy busy. My law practice has taken off." Kate felt the prolonged silence.

"Is it *really* your law practice?" Faith finally asked.

"Yes. Whose else would it be?"

"That's not what I meant. If it's your law practice keeping you busy, then I'm very happy for you. If it's some other chick, then I'm not so happy."

Kate could have kicked herself. How did she not see that coming? "Ah, no. I've been busy getting the practice set up, and I went to court with my first case this week. It's just been crazy."

"We have to celebrate. Let me take you to dinner Saturday night."

"Okay." Kate put her hand to her forehead and rubbed it.

"Great. Meet me at Marrino's in Southampton at eight o'clock."

"Okay." Kate laid her hand on the desk.

"I'll see you then." Faith hung up.

Kate held the receiver in front of her and stared at it for a moment. *What the hell is the matter with me?* Between preparing for Marjorie's case and visiting with Lane and Morgan over the weekend, Kate hadn't thought about Faith in days.

What about Faith? Do I want to see her? God knows she's hot and I could use a little fun. But what about Lane? We talked about taking it easy since she's just getting out of a relationship. Maybe I'm just some fun for her. I think I could have some real feelings for her, but at the same time, if she's not thinking along those lines, then there's no harm in seeing Faith. Amazing thing about being a lawyer, I could argue this either way. Have dinner with the hot chick. What harm could it do?

***

On Saturday, Faith was getting out of her car as Kate pulled into the parking lot of the restaurant. Faith waved when she spotted Kate and stopped to wait for her. Faith was wearing a short skin-tight dark raspberry colored dress with a black and raspberry pashmina over her shoulders.

"You look beautiful, as usual," Kate said as she joined her.

"Thank you." Faith linked her arm in Kate's. "You'll get to see more of me later."

Inside, they were seated in a cozy booth overlooking the water.

"What's new?" Kate asked after they got settled and ordered drinks.

"The usual summer activities: tennis, brunch, lunch, dinners, and social events. Some boring, some fun."

Kate was about to ask for details when a woman walked by the table and smiled at Faith and gently touched her shoulder.

"Past or current?" she asked.

"What does that mean?" Faith was not pleased.

"I was just wondering who she is."

"Someone from my social circle. And, for your information, I'm not seeing anyone but you."

"That's not what I was asking. It's okay if you want to see other people."

"Well, this is unusual for me, but I haven't wanted to see anyone but you."

"Really, Faith. It's okay. I mean what we have is just what we have, no commitments, just fun, right?"

"Well, I've been thinking about that, and I think we should examine the possibility of more."

Kate was speechless.

"I was thinking about staying out here for the fall and possibly the winter, depending on how things go. What do you think?" Faith said.

"I don't know. I mean, I don't want you to do anything that might jeopardize your current situation."

128

"You mean my husband? I don't think he would have a problem with me staying longer."

"It's up to you what you want to do, but I am beginning to get busy and might not be available."

"I'm sure I'll have plenty to keep me busy and we can see each other when we can."

"Why don't we take this one step at a time?" Kate was getting nervous.

"I think it's something you need to think about. I don't like to be disappointed. In the meantime, let's have a nice dinner and head back to my house."

"Sounds like a plan." Kate was flustered and couldn't think of anything else to say.

Later, after some good food and wine, Kate and Faith swam naked in the swimming pool before they had sex in the pool house, the gentle breeze blowing the curtains in rhythm with their swaying bodies. After they were fulfilled, they lay on the lounge, their skin glistening like the pool water reflecting the moonlight. Faith drifted off to sleep while Kate drifted off into her thoughts.

This can't work. How can it work? We really don't have anything in common. We don't have the same social circles. This was just supposed to be fun. I better start backing off. I'll be unavailable when she calls, and then she'll lose interest. She'll move on to someone else, and that will be it. Or, I could just tell her this is not going to work. Kate looked at the sleeping Faith. *I'll just back off and hope for the best. I'm such a chicken shit.*

Chapter Twenty-five

AND BACK OFF IS what she did. Over the next few weeks, Kate found herself in a happy routine of Friday night potlucks with the ladies and spending time with Natalie and Shannon at the Seagull, carefully avoiding Saturday nights. She was kept busy with new clients, spent two nights with Lane at a friend of Lane's house in Montauk, and managed to avoid Faith. Things seemed to be working out well.

One week before the historical society gala, Kate came downstairs to a kitchen buried in paperwork. She followed the trail along the counter and into the formal dining room where she found Constance, Patsy, and several other women preparing packets of information.

"Wow, ladies, it looks like you have quite a system going here."

Constance looked up from her pile of papers. "That's right, dear. We have this down to a science."

"Don't hang around too long, kiddo, or you'll get suckered in and never get out." Patsy waved a piece of paper at her.

"I don't mind. Is there anything I can do, Aunt Connie?"

"Don't worry, dear. I have plenty for you to do this week. I'll be needing help going over every detail of the event and making sure everything is on track. We'll need to go to the Manor House and check to make sure everything is being done there as well. Oh yes, dear, there will be plenty to do this week."

Kate's head was spinning. The event was Saturday evening, her parents and Lane were coming in on Thursday, and she had client meetings and a court case during the week. *Maybe I shouldn't have asked.* But busy was good, and Kate was sure it would be a great event.

Although Kate's parents had invited her, Kate had never attended the gala. She never felt old enough to go. More accurately, she felt it was a little more sophisticated than she was comfortable with. But now, with everything going well in her life, and feeling a little more grown up, she was looking forward to it.

Each night that week, she and Constance went to the Manor House to check on how the preparations were going. At one time, the Manor House was home to one of the original families on the island. Now, it housed the historical society and was open to catered affairs.

Constance met with other historical society members at the House and together they went over each detail. Kate hovered in the background and handled any tasks that were asked of her. Every night, something else happened to get ready for the gala. Tables and chairs were delivered and set up. The stage for the band was put together. On Wednesday, boxes of food, glassware, and wine arrived. By Friday night, the tables would be set up, and on Saturday, the fresh flower arrangements would be set out. Food preparation would start on Friday and continue through Saturday to assure that everything was fresh.

Thursday afternoon, Kate waited at the train station for her parents and Lane. They had coordinated their schedules so that they would arrive together. Kate got out of the car as the train rolled in and scanned the doors as they opened. A crowd poured out. Kate expected that many were there to attend the gala. She spotted her mom and dad, and Lane was just behind them. They were moving slow with all their luggage, trying to navigate the crowd.

Kate was surprised that the sight of her dad gave her a lump in her throat. She hadn't seen him in a few months. Overcome with emotion, she made her way toward the platform. When he caught sight of her, David set his luggage down and threw open his arms. Kate ran into his arms and would have knocked him over had he not swept her up and swung her around like he had done when she was a child. She clung to him while he spun her around.

"Oh, Dad, I've missed you," she cried.

"Hold on there. It's just your good old dad." His voice choked with emotion.

"Yes, who I've missed terribly."

"I've missed you too, sweetheart. Those phone calls just don't do it, do they?" He tightened his hug on her.

Kate gained control of herself to greet her mother and Lane. After collecting the bags, they headed for the car.

"Nice." David smiled as he got in the passenger seat.

"I know." Kate smiled.

After dropping Lane off at her grandmother's, Kate and her parents continued to Constance's house. David got out of the Range Rover and stood in the driveway. Kate and Morgan gave him a minute before they got out and stood alongside him.

"Boy, you don't realize how much you miss Belle until you come here." David shuffled his feet, but the distraction didn't work. Kate could see the tears in his eyes. Morgan put her arm around him.

"I know. But trust me, it only takes a moment, and then you can feel her all over the place."

"It's true." Kate nodded, looking at the house.

"Stop dallying and get up here." Patsy waved from the top of the pathway.

Constance had prepared cocktails and snacks on the patio, and Patsy led the way. After David and Morgan were greeted with hugs and kisses, the nonstop conversation began. David was questioned about everything he had done since the last time Constance and Patsy had seen him even though they received regular updates from Kate and Morgan.

A break in the conversation allowed Constance a chance to fill them in on her plans. "I have made reservations at the Rose and Thistle for dinner this evening. I've invited Lane and her grandmother, and of course Patsy will be joining us."

"Wouldn't be a good time without me." Patsy laughed.

Constance smiled at Patsy. "I wanted to cook you all a special dinner but with all the gala activity going on, I just don't have the energy".

"That's wonderful of you, Aunt Connie, but I think we all understand how busy you are right now." Morgan took hold of Constance's hand.

"Thank you, dear." Constance smiled. "Since you and David will be staying for the week, I promise to cook you some fabulous meals while you are here."

The lively conversation made the time pass quickly, and before Kate knew it, they were on their way to the restaurant. Laughter billowed out the car windows all the way through town. At the restaurant, they were shown to a table on the covered veranda. It wasn't long before Lane and Ellie joined them. Kate felt on top of the world being there with the people she loved most. She took Lane's hand and held it, smiling and hoping the night would never end.

Chapter Twenty-six

THE SMELL OF BACON woke Kate up. When she came down the backstairs to the kitchen, she found her father making pancakes and bacon.

"Morning, honey." David spun around still holding a spatula.

"What's up, Dad?" Yawning, Kate headed for the teapot.

"Your mother and Aunt Connie just finished eating some of my famous pancakes. I'm making a batch for you and me now."

"Are Mom and Aunt Connie gone already?"

"Yes. Don't you remember them going over the detailed plans last night?"

Friday had been a blur. Kate spent the morning with her father, showing him her office and driving around the island. After beers and a quick lunch at the Seagull, they picked Morgan and Constance up and took them to Patsy's for a pre-gala meeting. By the end of the evening, the only thing Kate knew for sure was that she needed to be ready to leave the house at five o'clock Saturday evening.

"I think I remember." She fixed her tea and sat down to watch her father. "They're at the Manor House with the rest of the ladies making sure everything is in order. They'll be back here at two to get dressed. We all leave at five so they can get back there to make sure everything they did this morning is still in order. They'll begin receiving guests at six-thirty for the cocktail hour, followed by the start of the dinner service at seven-thirty." Kate was startled at herself. "Wow. I guess I was paying attention."

David set a plate of pancakes in front of her. "No, honey, it was just repeated so many times it's implanted in your brain." He kissed the top of her head. "Anyway, it should be a great evening. It always is, but it will be even better this time because it will be the first one that you are attending. You will save a dance for your old dad, won't you?" He sat down with his plate of pancakes and the sides of bacon.

"Of course, I will. It's not like people will be standing in line to dance with me. Hey, do you think it would be okay if Lane and I danced together?" Kate asked as she had her fork of pancakes halfway to her mouth.

"I don't know, honey. I guess we'll have to check with Aunt Connie and see if she knows if there's a protocol for gay couples."

"Well, it's not like there aren't any gay people here on the island, especially in the summer. But I don't want to cause a scene. Aunt Connie will never let me hear the end of it if that happens. I'll check with Lane and see what she thinks too."

"So, you and Lane?" David crunched on some bacon.

"So, Lane and I are having a nice time together."

"And?"

"And she just got out of a bad relationship a few months ago, and I don't want to scare her off, so we are taking our time."

"But you like her?"

"I really like her." Kate grinned.

"Then you should let her know. Life is short. Sometimes you have to say what you feel."

"What was that?" Kate pointed her fork at David.

"What was what?"

"That was a Mom line."

"It was not." David reached for his coffee cup.

"It was too. You never say anything like that. In fact, you usually don't comment at all when it comes to anyone's love life, especially mine."

"I don't know what you're talking about." David smiled.

"Come on, Dad. What's the story? What did Mom put you up to?"

"Nothing."

"Really?"

"Look, if you tell her anything, I'll deny it all." David looked over his shoulder as if he were afraid Morgan would somehow catch him.

"Spill it."

"Your mother thinks you and Lane might be really good together and she didn't want to see you miss out on the opportunity. She thought that maybe if I encouraged you a little, you might not be so cautious."

"Cautious? I'm not cautious. I'm careful, and maybe I don't always follow through." Kate shook her head.

"Isn't that being cautious?" David picked up a piece of bacon and pointed it at Kate.

Kate grabbed her plate and headed toward the stove to grab more pancakes. For a moment, she thought about Faith.

"Well, as a matter of fact, this summer I did something that I was not careful or cautious about and had a really good time doing it."

"Okay, don't make me put my hands over my ears. I'm sure I don't want to hear the details."

"No, you don't." They both chuckled.

"You mother gave me an assignment. I did it, and made both of us uncomfortable, and I will include that in my report."

Kate set her plate down and wrapped her arms around her father's neck. "Make sure you get the story straight," she said as she kissed him on the cheek.

Promptly at two o'clock, Constance and Morgan arrived at the house. After a light lunch, they went to get ready for the next stage of the day. Kate and David sat on the patio playing cards until it was time for Kate to get ready.

Kate enjoyed listening to Constance and Morgan going back and forth between their rooms helping each other with hair, makeup, and dresses. When they offered to help Kate, she declined since she felt capable of getting ready on her own.

Since she had never attended the gala before, she felt like it was her coming out party, her introduction to the island's society set. People knew her as Belle's granddaughter and Constance's niece, but now that her practice was starting to thrive, she saw herself staying on the island, buying a home, making her life there. The gala was going to be the start of it.

After this evening, she would tell Constance, her parents, and Lane what her plans were. She would follow her mother and father's advice and tell Lane how she felt and what she planned and that she hoped Lane would want to be a part of those plans. Yes, tonight was going to be magical.

Chapter Twenty-seven

KATE LOOKED AT HERSELF in the mirror and imagined exactly how the evening would go. Her mother tapped on her bedroom door to let her know she and Constance were going downstairs.

"Okay," she said. "Down shortly. I have something to attend to first."

After a minute or two, Kate took a deep breath and went down the hall to her grandmother's room. After another deep breath, she stepped inside. The room was exactly how she remembered it. Decorated in various shades of pink and white, the wallpaper and the comforter on the bed were patterned with roses. She could still smell her grandmother's perfume in the air.

Kate made her way to her grandmother's vanity table and picked up the perfume bottle. As she held the precious liquid, Kate could feel her grandmother's presence and smiled to herself before spraying a mist of perfume into the air. As her smile grew, she stepped into the mist and coated herself in the flowery fragrance. Belle had taught her to do that when she was a little girl. She had never forgotten. As gently as she'd picked it up, Kate set the perfume bottle back on the vanity table and headed for the door. Before she stepped into the hallway, Kate turned and said, "I'll always love you, Gran." With little ceremony but great satisfaction and comfort, she stepped into the hall and pulled the door closed behind her and made her way downstairs.

"David, David come quick," Morgan gasped.

David hurried from the living room. "Holy smokes," he said, as he caught sight of Kate coming down the stairs.

"What's happened?" Constance asked as she followed David from the living room. She stopped in her tracks and put her hand to her mouth.

David took Kate's hand. "Wow. My daughter is always beautiful, but I have to tell you, honey, you look amazing."

"Thanks, Dad."

Morgan was in tears. "Look at you Kate. You look stunning. I'm speechless."

"Why, my dear, you are absolutely beautiful," Constance said.

For once, Kate agreed. She wore a dark rose strapless gown. Her hair was pulled up in the front and a handful of wisps cascaded softly in the back. Belle's ruby and diamond necklace glittered on her neck. Edward had given the necklace to Belle on their twenty-fifth wedding anniversary, and Belle had given it to Kate on her twenty-first birthday. Kate only wore it on special occasions.

"If I didn't know better, I'd have thought that was Belle coming down those stairs. Your resemblance to my sister is quite amazing." Constance choked back a sob. "She loved that color. And is that her perfume I smell?"

Kate tensed for a second. "I'm sorry, Aunt Connie. I should have asked you first."

Constance put her hand up. "No, my dear, you have every right and," Constance stifled another sob, "I'm so proud of you." Constance dissolved into tears along with Kate and Morgan.

David looked at the three women. "Ladies, you all look beautiful. This is a very emotional occasion, and I suggest, since I know you don't want to take a chance ruining your makeup, that you save this conversation for another time."

Morgan ran for the nearest box of tissues, and, without speaking a word, they collected themselves. David went to signal the limousine driver that they were ready. Between the two of them, they helped Kate, Morgan, and Constance into the car and left for the gala.

It was a beautiful summer evening and Kate felt like a princess. She looked out the window of the limousine as they drove down the almost two-mile-long driveway to the Manor House. She wondered what it must have been like to arrive in a horse drawn carriage years ago. As they got closer, Kate noticed the grounds staff lighting candle lanterns along the edges of the driveway. It wasn't quite dark yet, but it would be soon. Kate hoped she would get to see the lanterns lit later as they were leaving.

Before she knew it, the car door was opening and she, along with her mother and Aunt Connie, were being helped from the limousine. While everyone headed inside, Kate lingered to take in the scenery. The house was set on the highest point of the property and was surrounded by rolling hills, woods, and farmland. There was a beautiful view of the water in the distance. The evening air was filled with all the scents of the landscape. Huge flower arrangements flanked the large wooden doors and, above them, mounted to the outside walls, original oil lanterns burned brightly. As Kate made her way into the Manor House, she was greeted with more flower arrangements and soft music floating in the background.

"All right, everyone, you all have your assignments." Constance was dispensing last minute instructions. "Morgan and I will be at the reception table, and Kate, oh, there you are, my dear. You and your father will show people where their tables are. You have a little while before people start arriving, so you might want to take a walk around the ballroom and familiarize yourselves with the table arrangements. We will regroup at our table later."

"Okay, honey, let's look around." David took Kate by the hand. They made their way around the tables, stopping and looking at each table number to get an idea of the layout.

The ballroom boasted two huge stone fireplaces and high beamed ceilings. Windows overlooked gardens and provided gorgeous views of the water. Careful not to be caught by Constance, the two snuck into the hallway and peeked into some of the other rooms on the first floor. The rooms remained decorated in the fashion of the last lady of the manor, who had passed away some time ago. The rooms held the charm of the original house. The kitchen, currently bustling with activity, boasted a stone fireplace and a large wood farm table that could seat thirty people.

Not wanting to be discovered having abandoned their posts, Kate and David went back to the ballroom. Their timing was perfect as the first guests were just arriving. Kate and David gave each other a conspiratorial wink and took up their positions inside the doorway, prepared to escort the guests to their table.

Kate took great joy in greeting people. She recognized some of the guests, but others were new to the island and strangers to her. One of the newcomers was delighted to meet her. "So, you are Kate Whitfield. Marjorie Winters recommended you, and we'd like to come see you next week."

"Of course, give me a call and we'll schedule a meeting." Kate shook their hands and turned to greet the next guest.

Another newcomer spilled the beans about how Marjorie Winters came to be Kate's first client. Kate didn't know why she was surprised to find out that Aunt Connie had sent her. Later, Kate greeted Marjorie herself but didn't mention the clandestine referral. She chuckled as she decided she'd give Marjorie and Aunt Connie a hard time about that later.

Natalie and Shannon gave Kate a quick shout out as they ran by on the way to drop off last minute supplies to the kitchen staff. Still smiling after waving to Natalie and Shannon, Kate turned to greet more guests. That's when she saw her. Lane was a vision in an ice blue off-the-shoulder gown. Her blonde hair was curled softly and she wore a sapphire and diamond bracelet. Lane caught Kate's eye, waved, and made her way across the foyer.

"Oh, my God, you look beautiful!" She grabbed Kate's hand.

"So do you!" Kate sneaked a kiss on Lane's cheek.

"I thought we would never get here. My grandmother took forever."

"Isn't she on the greeting committee?"

"Please, she never gets on that one. That would mean she would have to be here early, which would take time away from getting ready and ruin her chance to make a grand entrance." Lane motioned over her shoulder. Sure enough, there was Ellie with a host of people in a circle around her.

"Well, she looks great."

"Your aunt didn't tell me anything about who is at our table, but I kept telling her without trying to be too obvious that you had to sit with me."

Kate laughed. "Yes, we're sitting with you and Patsy of course, as well as some of the other committee chairs and Richard Brodman and his wife. My friend Dex, his wife, and some of their friends are at another table."

"Is this the Dex who you told me about from college?"

"Yes."

"Has he ever attended this before?"

"He told me he usually has an event the same weekend but this year it was rescheduled. I'm excited he's coming." Kate smiled at Lane. "I'm looking forward to introducing you to him."

"Well, I am looking forward to a wonderful evening with you." Lane squeezed Kate's hand.

Kate looked into Lane's eyes. "I would like to talk to you about something very important."

"Is everything all right?" Lane looked concerned.

"That's just it. Everything is wonderful, and I want it to continue to be. That's why it's important that I talk to you." Kate looked around. The cocktail hour was in full swing.

"We can talk about that later but for now, let's get a glass of wine," Kate suggested. "I think my dad can handle greeting the last of the guests, and I have a minute or two before I need to start guiding people to the dining room."

"Okay, but just a quick glass. I have to make sure things are set for the auction."

Kate led Lane to the bar. After they each had a glass of wine, they went to tend to their assignments. People had started to move toward the dining room to find their seats. When Kate finally made her way to the table, everyone else was already seated. As Kate looked around the table, she noticed how elegant everyone looked—the men in their tuxes and the ladies in their gowns.

Richard and Victoria Brodman made a stunning couple. No wonder Dex was so handsome. Her parents looked so happy together. Constance was basking in the glow of the evening, and Patsy looked amazing in the gown she had told Kate earlier she had designed herself. She was chatting away with the women at the table next to her. Kate strained to see if she could spot Dex across the sea of tables, but she had no luck. After the meal and before the festivities got started, she would find him.

The meal was served and the conversations were easy and laughter filled the air. When the meal was cleared, people got up and began to socialize. The fundraising portion of the evening, including the auction would start just before dessert was served.

Kate leaned over to Lane. "I'm going to go find Dex. Do you want to come with me?"

"Absolutely. I have to get up and move or this dress is going to cut off my circulation."

Giggling, the two excused themselves and set off. Midway through the crowd, Kate spotted Dex coming towards her.

"Dex!" she called.

"There you are," he said pulling her into a hug. Stepping back and clasping Kate's hands, Dex gave her the once over from head to toe. "You look gorgeous."

"Why, thank you, and you don't look so bad yourself." He was more handsome now than he had ever been. They stared at each other for a few seconds until Lane cleared her throat.

"Hi. I'm Lane." She extended her hand to Dex.

Kate snapped back to reality. "I'm sorry, Lane. Dex, this is my girlfriend, Lane." She realized it as soon as she said it, but it was too late to take it back. She looked at Lane, who seemed a little surprised but she gave Kate a huge smile.

"It's a pleasure to meet you, Lane, and may I say you look beautiful?" Dex shook Lane's hand.

Kate beamed at Lane. "Doesn't she?"

"I'm sorry I haven't found you until now, but Judy and I came with some friends. One of the wives is always late so we ran in at the last minute."

Kate let him off the hook. "No big deal, Dex. We were busy anyway."

"Judy and her friends just went to the ladies' room, but why don't you come over to the table in a little bit and I can introduce you to everyone?"

"Sounds good. We'll see you in a little while." Kate reached out and gave Dex's hand a quick squeeze. She turned to lead the way back to their table, but Lane took her hand and guided her through one of the large wooden doors and out to the patio.

"That was an interesting introduction," Lane said.

Kate panicked a little. *Oh no, I've gone too far. Back pedal, Kate. Back pedal.*

"I'm sorry. I know we talked about not rushing things, so I apologize for that." As Kate watched the smile fade from Lane's face, she heard her father's voice encouraging her to be honest with Lane. "Actually, Lane, I'm not sorry. That's how I feel, which is why it just came out. It felt natural. I want you to be my girlfriend. I want us to start talking about a life together. I want..."

"Yes?" Lane smiled at Kate

"I want you." There. She said it.

Lane's eyes welled up with tears. She stepped close to Kate. "I want you too."

Kate wrapped her arms around Lane. "Don't cry. You'll ruin your make up and we will never hear the end of it from your grandmother."

Lane let out a little laugh. "Okay, okay," she said as she brushed away the last of her tears.

Kate took a step back and lifted Lane's chin with her finger. "This is what I wanted to talk to you about, but I suggest we discuss this later when we can be alone, okay?"

"Okay."

"One last thing now, though. You've made me very happy." Kate kissed Lane gently before taking her hand. "Ready?"

"Ready." Lane took a deep breath and the two went inside.

Kate and Lane returned to the table in time for the auction and dessert. After dessert, music filled the ballroom. "Do you want to dance? Do you think it will be okay?" Kate whispered to Lane.

Lane looked around. "I don't know. I've never thought about it before. I'm usually here alone."

"Who do we ask?"

Lane shook her head. "I feel like a kid in school again, afraid of doing something wrong and getting yelled at by the teacher."

"I could ask Patsy."

Lane laughed. "Oh, dear god, no. Don't ask Pasty. That's like asking a cigarette vendor if it's okay to smoke in the girl's bathroom."

"What about your grandmother?"

Lane got up and put her hand out. "Why don't we just dance?"

"Really?"

"Really."

Kate put her hand in Lane's, and Lane led her to the dance floor. On the floor, they each took a deep breath. "Here we go," Kate said with a chuckle. "Who's going to lead?"

She put her arm around Lane's waist. They started to sway with the music. After a few minutes Kate looked around. Nothing. No one was paying any attention to them. The music played and they danced until the song was over. "Well, no one threw anything at us, or screamed and fainted, so I guess we're okay." Kate smiled

"Or my grandmother is waiting until we get back to the table before she takes me by the ear and hauls me out of here."

"Would she do that?" Kate felt a twinge of anxiety.

"I don't think so. I mean, my grandmother and I have never discussed my sexual orientation. I know my mother told her I was gay so she wouldn't hear it from someone outside the family. But that was pretty much the extent of it."

"What was your grandmother's reaction?"

"She said she wanted me to be happy and hoped I would never get hurt."

"I'm sure she was none too pleased with what happened with your last relationship."

"No, not at all, which was why it was okay for me to come out here and stay after all that happened."

"Well, let's not ruin the moment with ugly thoughts. How about we go find Dex's table?"

"Sounds good."

They made their way through the crowd to the table where Dex, his wife, and their friends were seated. As they got close to the table, Kate saw her. Faith, glaring at her with a look that could melt steel. Kate stopped short, frozen in place. *What is she doing here? How did I miss her coming in? She must have arrived late. Oh my god. What am I going to do?*

Dex jumped to his feet when he saw Kate and Lane approaching. He dragged Kate by the hand to the table and started the introductions. After he introduced Kate and Lane to Judy, he got the attention of the table. He didn't seem to notice the look of discomfort on Kate's face.

"Friends, I would like you to all meet a very good friend of mine from college, Kate Whitfield. And this is her girlfriend, Lane Bellows. Ladies, I'd like you to meet, Paul and Joan Goodman, David and Diane Parker, and Peter and Faith Young."

Kate barely registered what Dex was saying. She vaguely heard Lane exchange pleasantries with the group. It sounded like everyone was talking in slow motion. Dex told his friends about how they met, how they recently reconnected, and how happy he was they could resume their friendship. Kate would normally have bantered back and forth with Dex, but all she wanted to do was get the hell out of there.

"You'll have to excuse us. Lane and I need to check to be sure we're not needed for any other duties this evening. It was so nice to meet you all."

"What's wrong?" Lane asked as soon as they were out of earshot of the table.

"I'm okay. I think I was having a hot flash or something. Why don't you go on to the table? I think I'll to go to the ladies' room and freshen up."

"Are you sure? I can come with you." Lane looked at Kate with concern.

"No!" Kate snapped. "I'm sorry, Lane. I just need a few minutes."

As they neared the table, Kate looked at her mother. As Kate sailed by the table, she overheard Morgan ask Lane what was wrong. Kate was in full stride as she made her way into the bathroom and into one of the stalls. She couldn't close the door fast enough. She put her hands on the back of the door after she locked it. She took one deep breath before her emotions got the best of her and the tears started. She was not prepared for this. Faith, who she was trying to avoid because she was too chicken to face her. Faith, with whom she might be in a relationship under different circumstances. Faith, who had warned her not to screw with her.

"Kate, I know you're in here."

Shit. It's Faith.

"I'm not leaving until you come out."

Great. Kate wiped her eyes. *I suppose this has to happen sometime. Here goes nothing.* She opened the door.

"Hello, Faith." Without the strength to fight, Kate came out of the stall, her shoulders slumped in defeat.

Faith turned and walked a few feet away and then turned to face Kate. "Well, well. Fancy meeting you here, as the saying goes."

"I know. Crazy, isn't it?"

"So, you've been so busy you haven't had time to see me?"

Okay, I can handle this. Kate straightened herself up

"It has been crazy, Faith. I really haven't had time for much of anything."

Faith took a step closer. "But you've missed me, right?"

Kate felt her body tingle with a sense of excitement. "Yes, of course."

Faith took another step closer and leaned in to whisper in Kate's ear. "You've been busy and you've been missing me, but yet you have a girlfriend?" She put her arms around Kate and pulled her closer. Kate felt the heat from her body, smelled her perfume. She felt like she was beginning to melt.

"How did that happen?" Faith pushed her back.

"It's not what you think, Faith." *What the hell am I saying? Tell her the truth.*

"Really? I'm not to think that all the while you're sleeping with me, you're not going around with that blonde introducing her to everyone as your girlfriend?" Faith's voice rose.

"I haven't been doing that."

"Have you been sleeping with her too?"

Kate didn't answer. Faith became enraged. "So, all this time that we've been together, you've been with her? All the times we talked about our feelings for each other, you've been romancing her? I've seriously thought about leaving my husband for you which, believe me, I've never thought of doing for anyone."

Faith closed in again. "And the one thing I asked you not to do was fuck me over. You were the one person I thought I could believe wouldn't do that to me. You, with all your concerns about what dreams I had and how I should be fulfilling my life. Tell me, Kate. Do you feed her the same lines?"

Kate was at a loss for words. For what felt like an eternity, she was silent. Finally, she swallowed hard. "Faith, I never meant to hurt you. I thought we could have something."

Faith was heading for the door. She stopped for a moment, her back still to Kate. "You know we have something, Kate, and I suggest you tell your little blonde girlfriend about it, or I will." And then she was gone.

Oh shit. I'd better get out there before Faith does something I'm going to regret. Kate didn't get farther than the ladies' room lounge. There they were. All of them staring at her, Morgan, Constance, Patsy, Ellie, and Lane. Lane was in tears. Lane turned and ran out of the bathroom before Kate could say anything. Ellie was right after her. Morgan grabbed Kate by the arm to stop her from following them.

"Honey, what in God's name is going on here?"

"Mom, I seriously can't talk right now. I have to get to Lane," Kate cried.

Kate pushed past her mother, ignoring the concerned looks from Constance and Patsy. Kate felt like everyone in the ballroom had heard the whole thing and was staring at her. She also felt like a complete shit. On her way out the door after Lane, Kate had to pass by Dex's table. Faith was nowhere in sight.

"Jesus, Kate, really?" Dex grabbed Kate by the arm and stopped her mid stride. "Faith? That's one of my best friends' wives. Judy heard what went on in the bathroom and came back and told me."

"You don't know what you're talking about. I need to get out of here." She shoved Dex out of the way and continued to the exit. When she was almost to the door, her dad wrapped his arms around Kate.

"Honey, what's wrong? What's going on?"

Kate opened her mouth to say something but couldn't get the words out.

"All right, let's get you out of here." David guided her outside to the car.

"What about Mom and Aunt Connie?" Kate asked.

"Not to worry, I'll call your Mom."

Kate began to sob. "Oh, Dad."

"It's okay. Let's just get you home."

Kate cried all the way home, into the house, and up to her room, her father by her side the entire time. Kate sat on the edge of the bed and hung there like a deflated balloon. She kicked off her shoes and punched the bed with two fists. David kissed her on the top of the head and gave her hand a quick squeeze.

"It will all be better in the morning," he said as he closed the bedroom door.

Kate didn't believe that for a second. Still crying, she threw herself back on the bed. A few minutes later, she heard a car come up the driveway. *Great. Mom and Aunt Connie are going to come read me the riot act now.* Sure enough, Morgan tapped on the door and called to Kate, but she didn't answer. When she could cry no longer, she fell asleep.

Chapter Twenty-eight

KATE AWOKE THE NEXT morning hoping the prior evening had been a bad dream. The sight of her mother sitting in the window seat told her it wasn't. She started to cry again as Morgan came to the bed and cradled her.

"There, there, my darling, just get it out."

Kate cried harder, but abruptly stopped.

"Mom, I have to go see Lane."

"Oh, dear."

"What?"

"Lane left the island. Aunt Connie spoke to Ellie this morning."

"What? I have to talk to her." Kate pulled away from Morgan.

Morgan got up and poured them both a cup of tea from the tray she had placed on the nightstand. "It might be a good idea for you to give her a little time and for you to collect yourself."

"Oh, dear god. How much did you all hear?" Kate put her hands to her face.

"Pretty much everything, I guess. I knew something was wrong when you passed the table. Then when Lane said you needed a few minutes, I thought you might be ill or something, so I followed you to the bathroom. When I heard you talking to that woman, I waited in the lounge and the next thing I knew, Constance, Patsy, Lane, and Ellie were with me."

"So, you all heard everything?" Kate shook her head.

Morgan nodded. "Aunt Connie and Patsy made sure Lane and Ellie got on their way while your father brought you home. Then Aunt Connie, Patsy, and I worked to see if we needed to do any damage control."

"How much damage control was there to do?"

"Not much really. We shooed away the busy bodies and Aunt

Connie and Patsy talked to Dex for a minute. Patsy recognized the woman as a guest at Dex's table from earlier in the evening."

"Oh, dear god. Dex," Kate said under her breath.

"The woman wasn't at the table when they got there, though, and Dex told them she had gone home. The rest of the evening went on like nothing happened."

Morgan sat on the bed with Kate. "Are you ready to tell me what's going on?"

"It's a long story."

"We have time."

Kate told Morgan everything, minus a few intimate details. "What do you think, Mom?"

"I think you need to look good and hard at what you want out of life and whether or not either one of these women can give it to you or…" Morgan got up and walked back to the tea tray.

"Or what?"

"Or if you need to move on and find someone else. Now," Morgan picked up the tray, "you must be hungry. Why don't you come downstairs? Breakfast is on the table."

"I can't go down there." Kate pulled the blankets over her head.

"Why not?"

"Aunt Connie."

"Just another woman with whom you need to work things out," Morgan said. "Besides, I think you have a better chance talking with your Aunt Connie than with Lane or that other one." Morgan closed the door behind her.

What the hell am I going to do? Kate headed for the shower. She stopped short when she caught a glimpse of herself in the mirror. At some point, she had managed to take her evening gown off. Mascara streaked her face. Her disheveled hair was still pinned up in places and hung down in others. *Dear god*, Kate thought, *I look like a deranged princess. Better get myself cleaned up.* Kate stepped in the shower before the water warmed up. Standing there, with the cold water pouring down on her, she cried some more. As the water began to heat up, Kate pulled herself together. When she finished getting dressed, Kate took a deep breath and headed downstairs.

At the bottom of the stairs, Kate heard her parents talking to Aunt Connie and Patsy. She hesitated a moment before she walked into the kitchen.

"Morning kiddo. How you doing?" Patsy squeezed the daylights out of her.

"Morning, Pats. I'm okay." Kate hugged her tight.

"There you are, dear." Constance got up from the table and walked over to her.

"Aunt Connie, I'm so sorry." Kate collapsed in tears and stepped forward to hug Constance.

"What's this? You have no reason to apologize." Constance returned Kate's hug.

"Yes, I do". Kate stepped back to look at Constance. "You allowed me to come here and now I've hurt your friend and ruined your gala." Kate sobbed harder.

Constance gathered Kate into another hug. "You have been nothing but a pleasure. You did not ruin the gala, and as far as hurting anyone, I believe that it's you that's hurting the most." Constance ran her hand down the back of Kate's head. "Now, I want you to sit down. You're going to have some tea and something to eat, and then we are going to decide what's best for you to do next. All right?"

Kate nodded and sat down.

"I think it's best that you call Lane. She might hang up on you, but at least try. If she talks to you, terrific. If she doesn't, then you must decide what your plan is from there. As for the other woman...what is her name, dear?" Constance poured a cup of tea and handed it to her, along with a tissue.

"Faith."

"All right then, as for Faith, it seems like she's a trouble maker. We may have to neutralize her." Constance returned to the teapot to pour herself a cup.

"Neutralize her?" Morgan said. "Sounds a little criminal."

"Good," David said with a chuckle. "I thought I was the only one concerned about that."

"Hey, what you don't know won't hurt you." Patsy shook her scone at David.

"Constance and Patsy, undercover assassins." Now Morgan was chuckling.

"All right, you two, this is serious," Constance said, ending the frivolity. "Now, dear, could this woman cause you any trouble?"

"I don't know. I know she isn't happy with me right now, but do anything? I don't know what she could do." Kate shrugged.

"Then the first thing we have to do is to find out what she's capable of. Patsy, make a few phone calls and see what you can find out,"

Constance said.

"I'm on it. What's her last name and where does she live, kiddo?"

"Young. Southampton." Kate rubbed her face with her hands.

"I'll be back." Patsy took her tea and scone and headed for the living room.

"I suggest we wait and see what Patsy turns up and go from there. Kate, once you've calmed down a little more, go call Lane. That way you know what you're dealing with as far she's concerned." Constance patted Kate's hand and went to join Patsy.

David got up and poured himself more tea. "I don't know about you two, but I'm a little more afraid of Constance now than I was before."

"I wouldn't put anything past those two," Morgan admitted.

Kate started to laugh.

"What's so funny, dear-heart?" Morgan asked.

"I was picturing those two blindfolding Faith and throwing her in the trunk of a car." Kate laughed harder.

"And taking her to some deserted warehouse and interrogating her." Morgan grinned.

"Will they get the information they want and turn her loose or..." David sinister voice impression drifted off, the question unfinished.

After a moment, in unison they said, "Nah." And then they erupted in laughter.

Moments later, Constance and Patsy returned. "Looks like we might be in for some trouble." Patsy said, plopping herself down at the table. "Turns out this Faith has caused issues for some people."

"Like what?" Morgan asked.

"Seems she has broken up a few marriages. She gets involved with someone's wife, and then, when things don't work out, she pulls the old society blacklist routine." Patsy held up a piece of paper that she had made some notes on.

"Well, it's certainly not like Kate's a society target." Morgan got up and paced the kitchen.

"But her family is." Patsy tapped her finger on the table. "Morgan, you're a famous artist. David is a well-known doctor. Constance and I are social icons."

"You, Pats?" David said.

"Guilty by association."

"She can't harm any of our reputations, can she?" Morgan was still pacing.

"She mostly certainly can. And she can hurt Kate's reputation too, and destroy her business. That's why we have to find a way to neutralize her." Patsy slapped her hand on the table.

"Patsy, would you stop saying that? You're starting to creep me out." Kate again pictured Faith blindfolded in the trunk of a car. She shook the image from her mind.

"First things first, my dear, you have to call her. If she's the type I think she is, she'll show her hand by telling you what she's going to do to you." Constance stood next to Kate's chair.

"Great. That sounds promising." Kate put her head on the table.

"Once she does that, we'll know how to proceed." Constance put her hand on Kate's shoulder.

"Be brave, kiddo. We've got you covered," Patsy said.

"Come, Patsy. We must be off to the Manor House to clean up from last evening. Morgan? David? We could use some help."

"I think we should stay here with Kate," Morgan said.

Constance motioned with her hand for Morgan and David to come with her and Patsy. "I think Kate has some things to think about and do on her own."

"She's right, Mom. You guys go ahead. I'll be all right."

"Are you sure?" Morgan asked.

"Yes. Go on, and when you all get back, I'll give you an update."

"All right, but you call if you need us." Morgan and David each gave Kate a kiss and left with Patsy and Constance.

Kate put her head on the table again and let out a big sigh. "What have I done?"

It took a good five minutes before Kate could pull herself together enough to look for her cellphone. She placed it on the table and then picked up it up and set it back down with a sigh. Once again, she picked up the phone and set it back down. Another sigh. The third time she picked it up, she forced herself to dial Lane's number. *Oh, my god, it's ringing.* Kate's heart was racing. On the fourth ring, the line was picked up but nothing was said. Kate was sure anyone other than Lane would have said hello.

"Lane, is that you?" Kate heard a sniffle. "Lane, I'm so sorry. I need to explain. It's not what you think. Yes, there was something going on with me and Faith, but I had stopped seeing her and I wanted to talk to you to last night about the plans I have for you and me. Please, Lane, you have to let me explain." Kate started to cry.

Through more sniffles, Lane said, "I need time."

"Time? I can give you time. Not too much time, I hope?" Kate knew she sounded desperate.

Lane hung up, but Kate continued to hold the phone to her ear and cry. When she started to calm down, she set the phone on the table. *Maybe needing time is a good sign. She wants to think about things. When she calms down, then we can talk. Or,* Kate tortured herself, *she won't believe me and she'll just think I've hurt her like her last lover did. Then of course she'll just hate me and it will be over. End of story.*

Kate's heart ached at the thought of having hurt Lane so deeply. She sat at the table for another few minutes before she could make her next call. Each number she pressed was more painful than the previous one. Kate waited for the phone to ring.

"Well, well," Faith sneered, "look who we have here."

"Faith, look, it's not what you think."

"You think I'm stupid, Kate? Not what I think? I'll tell you what I think. I think you've messed with the wrong person."

"Faith, listen to me," Kate pleaded.

Faith cut her off. "No, you listen to me. I told you from the start not to fuck with me, and I hope you're prepared for the consequences."

"Faith, meet me somewhere and let me explain."

"Yeah, I don't think so. I think you better start thinking about moving because when I'm done with you, nobody is going to give you the time of day let alone hire you as their lawyer." With that, she hung up.

Kate pulled the phone away from her ear and stared at it for a moment as if doing so would change the outcome of the call. "Well, that went well." Kate poured another cup of tea and moved into the living room where she dozed on the couch until she heard everyone return. She went back to the kitchen and they all gathered at the table.

"Well?" Morgan asked.

"Well," Kate said, "Lane needs time."

"That's a good sign, dear." Morgan patted Kate's hand.

"And Faith, well Faith apparently is going to make my life miserable by destroying any business opportunities I may have."

"Crap. I knew it." Patsy smacked her hand on the table.

"Now, let's not get too excited. We don't know what that means," David said.

"What are you thinking, Connie?" Patsy asked.

Constance put her finger to her lips, tapped them a few times. "I think Kate should keep calling Lane until she will listen to what Kate has to say."

"And the other one?" Patsy stood up and moved close to Constance so she could hear what Constance had to say.

"She needs to be neutralized," Constance whispered to Patsy.

Kate caught the last sentence. *Did I hear that right?*

Constance quickly covered her comment to Patsy. "We will figure out how to handle the other one. In the meantime, Kate, you need to go about your business as usual. We will discuss this again in the middle of the week and see where we are."

Chapter Twenty-nine

OVER THE NEXT FEW days, between bouts of crying, Kate managed to go to the office and get some work done. Surprisingly, everything seemed to be quite normal. Phone calls were coming in, and cases were getting booked. By Wednesday, Kate needed a break. She decided to ride her bike to the Seagull for a drink. Before she went inside, she checked the cars in the area to make sure Faith wasn't lying in wait for her. After scoping the small crowd, Kate took a seat at the end of the bar. Before she knew it, a beer appeared before her.

"Should I keep them coming?" Shannon asked and patted Kate's hand.

Natalie and Shannon had somehow heard what had happened and Natalie had called Kate to let her know.

"Thanks, Shannon. No. One is probably good. I just need a break."

"You doing okay?"

"I'm okay. Has anyone been around asking for me?" Kate looked around the bar.

"Not a soul. We would have called you if we didn't think it was safe."

"I appreciate that." Kate took a sip of the beer. "Where's Natalie?"

Before Shannon could answer, Natalie appeared from the kitchen and sat on the barstool next to Kate. "Oh my God, are you okay? I wanted to call again but I thought I should wait until things settled down. And now here you are. What do you need? Can we do anything?"

"I'm okay."

"Really?" Natalie sounded surprised. "I think I'd be hiding out after hearing what Faith might be capable of doing."

Kate sipped her beer. "I guess I have what's coming to me. I'll deal with the fallout from Faith. It's Lane that has me worried."

Natalie moved her barstool in closer. "Do tell."

"I really want to be with Lane, but I think I've ruined any chance of that."

"I heard she left Sunday morning. Have you spoken to her?" Natalie asked.

"I called."

"And?" Natalie probed.

"And she picked up the phone, listened to me, and then said she needed time."

"That's a good sign, don't you think?" Natalie patted Kate's hand.

"Maybe, but she just ended a relationship with someone who cheated on her, and now that's what it looks like I was doing. I'm not sure what she's thinking."

"It seems to me that Lane is pretty sensible and will come around and see how it really is." Natalie nodded.

"What about Faith?" Shannon asked. "Any interest in her?"

"Shannon. Really? Kate wouldn't have any interest in Faith," Natalie said.

"Calm down, Nat. I'm just asking." Shannon held up her hands in surrender.

"It's okay, Natalie. Honestly, there are several reasons why that could or couldn't have worked. I'm a lawyer. I could argue it either way. Under the right circumstances it might have worked."

No!" Natalie gasped.

"You know," Shannon said, "when Faith came in and wasn't on the make, was just being herself, she was pretty cool. But then she would do a one-eighty and become a royal pain in the ass."

"Probably a good description," Kate agreed.

"Okay, you two. I'm obviously missing something that you see in her, because I think she's a pain in the ass. But that's just me. What's your plan, Kate?" Natalie sounded a little worried.

"Work and drink and work and drink. No, that's not true. I guess I'll wait for a little while and call Lane again to see if she'll talk to me. I'd like to talk to Faith too, as long as she doesn't attack me in some way first."

"Good luck with that," Natalie said.

"You'll be fine, Kate," Shannon said as she made her way to the kitchen. "Hang in there."

Kate put a ten on the counter. "I guess I'm going to head back home now."

Natalie smacked her hand. "You take that back. We got you

covered on this."

"Thanks, Nat." Kate gave her a hug. "Let me know if you hear of any trouble coming my way."

"You know we will."

Kate rode her bike home. Twilight was falling as she rode up the driveway. She thought of nothing besides Lane the entire ride. Candlelight from lanterns around the patio told Kate where everyone was gathered for the evening. After putting her bike in the garage, she headed up the path to the patio. As Kate got closer to the patio, she could see only one figure in the shadows.

"Aunt Connie?"

"Hello, dear. Did you have a nice ride?"

"Yes. Where are Mom and Dad?"

"They took a walk down the beach. Beautiful evening, isn't it?"

Kate sat down. "Yes, it is."

Constance turned to look at her. "Kate, dear, I need to talk to you."

Kate's heart started to pound. *Oh god, here it comes. We're going to talk about the incident again even though she said everything was fine. I knew it wasn't.* "Is everything all right, Aunt Connie?"

"Yes, dear. But there's something you and I need to get settled. No, that's not really what I mean to say." Constance seemed at a loss for words and even a little uncomfortable.

"What is it, Aunt Connie?"

Constance took a deep breath. Kate also took one.

"Your grandmother always had a way of making everything all right, no matter how bad it seemed. She always knew what to do. I wish she were here now to help you because I'm feeling a little helpless at the moment."

"Aunt Connie, you've been wonderful." Kate leaned forward in her chair.

"Well dear, you and I both know we have never really been close. You and your grandmother, yes, but us, not so much. I hope, though, that you know I love you."

"Of course, I do." Kate wasn't sure where the conversation was going, but she was sure she didn't like it. "Are you okay, Aunt Connie?"

"Oh dear, yes, of course I am. I'm just fine. I'm sorry, dear. I'm not doing this very well. Let me try again." Constance cleared her throat. "I know I can't help you like your grandmother could, but I think I have something that may help." Constance produced an envelope from her lap and handed it to Kate.

To Kate. Kate recognized her grandmother's handwriting. "What's this?" Kate stared at the envelope.

"It's a letter from your grandmother. Would you like to stay here and read it? I can go inside."

For a moment, Kate couldn't think.

"No Aunt Connie. You stay here."

"Fine, dear. I'll be sitting out here for a while if you need me."

Kate got up and went inside. She stopped in the kitchen, not sure where to go to read the letter. After a moment, she turned and went upstairs to her grandmother's bedroom. She walked to the window and turned on a small lamp by the window seat. With trembling fingers, she opened the letter.

My dear darling Kate,

First and foremost, I want you to know how much I love you. You have been one of the greatest joys in my life, along with my beloved Edward and my children. I have always tried to do the best for all of you. As such, I have made sure that you always feel my love.

If I haven't given it to you already, I have made it known to all that you shall receive my Mercedes. I bought it the year you were born, and it has always brought me much pleasure. It's yours now. A trust has also been set up for you. You will inherit the bulk of my estate, including Belle's Beauty, all of its contents, and my boat, Belle's Waterlily. Only you feel the same as I do about this island and what we have here. Only you will continue as I would have. And for these reasons, I give you these things. Please do not worry about the rest of the family. They have all been well provided for.

One last thing, my dear Kate. It is my hope that you and your Aunt Connie will form a friendship. Please know that she loves you very much and always has.

All my love,
Gran

Tears flowed down Kate's cheeks as she read the letter again and again. *This can't be. How? I can't.* Kate sat in silence for a few more minutes as the words sunk in. She rejoined Constance on the patio. She was in the same spot Kate had left her. Without a word, Kate sat down beside her.

"This can't be possible, can it?" Kate looked at Constance.

Constance took Kate's hand. "I know it seems a little overwhelming, but yes, it's true."

"But why? I don't understand."

"You and your grandmother are very much alike—headstrong, passionate, and sensitive. She wanted to make sure that you had all the tools you needed to make a difference like she always tried to do. She felt the best tool she could leave you was her legacy."

"But what about you? What about everyone else?"

"Oh, my dear. We have all been taken care of. Belle made sure none of us will ever have to worry."

"What happens now?"

"There is some paperwork you need to sign, transfer of funds and deeds and all that, but that's about it. Everything is in Richard's office waiting for you. He will come over whenever you are ready and take care of it all." Constance hesitated a moment. "Then I'll make plans to move out."

"What?" Kate jumped to her feet. "You can't leave, Aunt Connie. This is your home."

"It has been my home, but now it's yours, dear, and you'll want to make it your own."

"No, Aunt Connie. I'm not changing a thing, and you're not leaving." Kate fell to her knees and buried her head in Constance's lap, sobbing. "You can't leave me here."

Constance patted her head. "It's all right, dear. It's all right. Well then, if you'll have me, I'll stay for the time being."

Kate lifted her head. "Time being? As in forever, right?"

"Let's take one step at a time, all right?" Constance wiped the tears from Kate's face with a tissue. Kate wondered how it was that old people always seemed to have a tissue handy when one was needed. She managed a little smile. Kate had barely settled in her chair when Morgan and David returned from their walk.

"Everything all right?" Morgan asked.

"I think we're going to be just fine." Constance reached over and cupped Kate's face with one hand. "What do you think?"

Kate smiled through watery eyes. "I think we are going to be perfect."

Chapter Thirty

TO KATE'S RELIEF, MORGAN and David decided to stay on the island until after Richard Brodman helped transfer ownership of Belle's estate to Kate. It rained the morning he was scheduled to come, so lunch, catered by The Rose and Thistle, would be served in the sunroom rather than on the patio. Kate stood in the sunroom and watched the raindrops bounce off the patio table. Even on the dreariest of days, the view of the harbor was spectacular. Nearby, two servers moved about the table setting up for lunch. In the kitchen, another Rose and Thistle employee prepared the food. To Kate, it almost felt like the day of Belle's funeral. Wait staff, servers, cooks, all sorts of people in the house waited on the throngs of people that came to pay their respects. She shook off the feeling and continued to look out over the water.

"There you are. I've been looking all over for you." Morgan came and stood behind her.

"You found me." Kate sighed.

"There, there, dear-heart. This is a happy occasion."

"Is it?"

"Well, it should be. Your grandmother intended it to be."

Kate turned around. "You know, Mom, you could have prepared me for this."

"What do you mean?" Morgan looked puzzled.

"I mean, you all knew about this and nobody bothered to tell me or give me a hint."

"It wasn't our place to tell, directly or by giving you a hint." Morgan lifted her hand to touch Kate's cheek.

"Why not?"

"Because it is a gift from your grandmother. It was important that you learn about it from her, whether she was able to tell you in person or not."

"I guess I can understand that," Kate conceded.

"Of course, your grandmother has been preparing you for this from

165

the day you were born."

"Okay, now you've lost me."

"From the moment your grandmother first held you, she knew you were going to be like her and from then on she wanted to share her world with you."

"How?"

"Every place she took you and everything she showed you were all places and things she loved. The opera, the Broadway shows, the museums, the social events. She wanted to see if you would love it as much as she did."

"I still do, although I haven't had much time for all of it."

"You even became a lawyer. You didn't know it, but your grandmother would have loved to have studied law." Morgan laughed. "She used to drive Richard crazy going over every detail. Do you remember what your grandmother bought you for your tenth birthday?"

Kate thought for a moment. "The bike I wanted so badly and a little leather briefcase."

"That's right. The bike for riding with her in the preserve and the briefcase for playing office."

"I remember it wasn't long before I started taking the briefcase to school." Kate smiled.

"Oh yes. When your teacher asked you about it, you explained that you were going to be a lawyer. Your teacher was impressed with your ambition."

Kate looked around the sunroom. It was large, almost the length of the house. She glanced at the table and counted eight place settings. "Who all is coming to lunch?"

"Um, well," Morgan studied the table as she thought aloud, "you, your father and me, your Aunt Connie and Richard, and Patsy of course."

"There are two additional place settings." Kate counted again.

Morgan seemed puzzled as well.

"I guess we'll find out soon enough," Morgan said.

"So where is everyone?" Patsy bellowed from the kitchen.

"Lovely day for a duck, wouldn't you say?" Patsy joined Morgan and Kate in the sunroom. They each planted a kiss on her cheek. "What's with the long faces? You'd think someone died." She laughed out loud. "That's right, someone did."

"Really, Patsy, making jokes?" Constance came in behind her,

"What? This is a good occasion that has occurred because someone did die, and now someone else is going to benefit from it."

"That just sounds so wrong." Kate shook her head.

"Come on, kiddo, your grandmother meant this to be a good thing, and it is, so let's lighten the mood a little. Constance, is there champagne?"

"What do you think?"

"Oh, goody. I'll go get that girl, what is her name? The one who always waits on us?"

"Debbie."

"That's it. Debbie. I never can remember her name. I'll go find Debbie," she said accentuating the name, "and have her bring us out a round."

Kate heard her father talking to someone and moments later he escorted Richard and Dex into the sunroom. Kate's heart skipped when she saw Dex. The last time she spoke to him was at the gala when he confronted her about Faith. His presence explained one of the extra place settings.

"Good afternoon, ladies." Richard took Kate's and Morgan's hands. "I've brought Dex along to help today since we have a good number of things to get through."

"What a wonderful idea," Morgan said. "It's good to see you again, Dex."

"Champagne is on its way," Patsy announced as she entered the sunroom.

Dex made his way over to Kate. "Hi."

"Hi." Kate could feel her body start to tense up a little.

"Look, Kate, I need to talk to you. Will you give me a few minutes when this is done?"

"Sure." She smiled, trying to shake the tense feeling.

He smiled and returned to his father's side.

"Richard, I expect that we are all set. I have scheduled lunch for an hour from now to give us time to get through the paperwork. Will that work for everyone?" Constance asked.

"As long as I have champagne, I will gladly wait for lunch," Patsy said. Everyone laughed as they took their seats.

Richard cleared his throat and began as Dex passed each person a packet of paperwork. "As you all know, we are here today to formally execute the estate of Arabella Morgan Hilliard Whitfield. Immediately upon Belle's death, separate arrangements were made to disperse to her children, Morgan and Niles, her sister, Constance, non-family members, and organizations what she had bequeathed to them. All that paperwork has been filed and finalized. It was at Belle's request that the rest of her estate be dispersed to the designated beneficiary, Katherine Arabella Whitfield, when Constance, or in Constance's absence, Morgan, felt the time was right. This time having arrived, we begin."

For almost an hour, Kate signed or initialed page after page as she accepted each item. With each page, reality started to sink it. Her grandmother really had left her everything—the house and all its contents, the boats, the stocks, the bank accounts, the investments. She was glad that Debbie had refilled their champagne glasses while they completed the paperwork. She was certain it helped her keep herself together.

When they were done, Morgan and Constance signed the final decree of transfer and Patsy witnessed it. Richard had previously collected a signature from Kate's Uncle Niles, who was traveling on business and unable to be present for the proceedings.

Constance signaled for Debbie who brought another bottle of champagne to the table as she stood up. "I'd like to make a toast." Everyone raised their glasses. "To Kate, who like her grandmother before her, loves this home and this island and who will do her best to carry on all the good will that Belle so loved to do."

"Hear, hear," was the collective response as they clicked glasses.

"May I say something?" Kate asked.

"Of course," Constance said.

Kate took a deep breath and stood up. "First of all, I have to say that this is completely overwhelming and unexpected. I came out here to find my way after my life fell apart in Manhattan. Everything I knew to be true in my life had disappeared. But the one thing that has remained true from the moment I got here, as it always has before, is that this home, this island and the people I have here, heal my heart and soul like no other place ever could. I have always thought that I would eventually live here, that I would make my way in life and find a way to be here. And with help from my family, that can happen now. I want each one of you to know—Mom, Dad, Aunt Connie, Patsy—that I love you more then you could ever know, and I thank you so much."

By the time Kate finished speaking, there wasn't a dry eye at the table. Kate went around the table and hugged each one of them. Swept up in the moment, she hugged Richard and Dex as well.

"All right, I think it's time we have something to eat." Constance directed everyone to a nearby table where servers were beginning to fill the water glasses. Lunch was ready. As they took their seats, Kate's attention was again drawn to the number of place settings.

"Who else are you expecting, Aunt Connie?"

"No one dear. I must have miscounted." Without another word, Constance moved to the head of the table and took her seat.

"What was that?" Kate looked at Patsy. "Aunt Connie doesn't miscount when it comes to seating arrangements."

"I don't know what you're talking about so don't ask me." Patsy escaped to her chair

Something was going on. Kate was sure of it. She shrugged it off and sat down.

Half way through lunch the rain stopped. Soon, the clouds started to break up, and the sun began to emerge. The energy in the room increased accordingly.

Dex gave Kate a quick tilt of the head. Kate excused herself and Dex followed suit. The two wandered out onto the patio and soaked up a minute of sun.

"I want to apologize for my behavior at the gala. I was caught off guard by what went on with you and Faith, and I didn't handle it as well as I should have."

"How did you know what was going on? I didn't think we were that loud."

"Judy had gone into the ladies' room and caught some of the exchange between you and Faith. It was enough for her to get the idea of what was going on."

"Does Faith's husband have *friends* as well?"

"Yes, and sometimes when we go out and run into one of them, it gets uncomfortable. I respect that Faith and Peter have their special arrangement, but when it turned out that you were in the mix, it was a little much for me." Dex put on his best puppy dog eyes. "Forgive me?"

Kate never could resist them. "Of course, I do." Kate hugged him.

"Good. And for the record, Faith really can be a nice person."

Kate smiled. "Yes, she can be. Which is why I really could have fallen for her. But she's also such a handful."

"Ah, so the fair Lane captured your heart instead?"

"Yes, but I'm pretty sure I blew it." Kate's smile disappeared.

"Are you sure?"

"She said she needed time. But I'm not feeling too hopeful. I know I really hurt her."

Dex took Kate's hand and kissed it. "Time does heal, Kate, but sometimes people need more than just time. I wouldn't let too much time pass or you may lose her completely."

"Thanks, Dex." Kate hugged him again before they joined the rest of the group for dessert.

Chapter Thirty-one

THE NEXT DAY, AFTER her parents left the island, Kate and Constance settled back into their usual routines with one major exception. Constance now explained how things were handled around the house. She made sure Kate understood not only the day-to-day aspects of running the house but also the procedures for general maintenance and repairs. Even though Constance had an accountant to handle bills and other financial obligations, she kept a close eye on the books and encouraged Kate to do the same.

At first Kate felt uneasy probing into what she considered Constance's business, but the more that Constance reminded her that this was hers now, the more she realized the need to pay attention and be informed. Still, she knew that Constance wasn't going anywhere any time soon, and this gave her unspoken permission to slack a little. She knew she would get the hang of things in due time. In the meantime, Kate concentrated on her work, social obligations, and trying to win Lane back, whom she called every few days. Lane never answered, but Kate always left the same message, "Hi Lane. I miss you and I want to be with you. I hope you are all right."

Kate was not looking forward to the first potluck after the gala. She cringed at the thought of seeing Ellie Bellows even though Constance and Patsy assured her everything would be okay. But Ellie didn't attend the potluck. When Ellie didn't attend the next one either, Kate was distraught, fearing she had ruined the friendship between Constance and Ellie. Constance dismissed Kate's concerns without explanation, and Patsy was no help either. Kate tried not to let it bother her, but occasionally her mind would wander and she would worry about it.

She was thinking about it, sitting at her desk in the office when her cell phone rang. Without checking the caller ID, she answered, "Hello. This is Kate." No response. "Hello?" Nothing. Kate hung up. She checked the call log and found the call was from a private number with no further information. *Could it be Faith?* Given the recent events, it was unlikely that Faith would be calling. She contemplated calling Faith to apologize, but Kate thought better of waking the sleeping lioness.

Kate tapped her pen on her desk. "My god, what's become of me?" *I'm afraid of Lane, I'm afraid of Ellie Bellows, I'm afraid of Faith. All for different reasons but since when have I ever been so afraid of something that I haven't been able to confront it?*

Kate slammed her pen down on the desk. Her feet barely touched the stairs on the way to her car. Kate's first stop was the Bellows' residence. As she pulled into the driveway, her bravado weakened and her pulse increased. She hesitated in the car for a moment before forcing herself to walk to the front door. She raised her hand to knock but then let it drop to her side. It would have been easy to turn around and leave. Instead, Kate raised her arm again and knocked on the door. When no one answered, Kate convinced herself she'd tried and turned to leave but stopped herself before she got down the first step. *That's lame,* she thought. *It's a big house. She's probably either on her way to answer the door or didn't hear me. I can do this.* Kate's fortitude returned. She pivoted on her heels and rang the doorbell. After a moment, the door opened.

"Kate, I wasn't expecting you." Ellie smiled.

"Hi. Can I speak to you for a moment, please?"

"Of course, dear. Would you like to come in?" Ellie opened the door wider.

"I would if that's okay." Kate was surprised at how friendly she seemed.

Ellie motioned for her to come in. "Come into the kitchen, dear. I have something on the stove."

Kate followed her through the house to the kitchen.

"Please, have a seat. May I offer you something to drink?"

"No, thank you. I'm sorry. I don't mean to interrupt. I just needed to speak to you." Kate pulled out a stool from under the center island and sat down.

"Let me just give this pot a quick stir, and then you can have my undivided attention." Ellie turned to the stove before sitting across the island from Kate.

"Doctor Bellows, I want to apologize for what happened at the gala. I know how hard you work every year, and I hate to think that I did anything to upset that. But most important, I must apologize for hurting

Lane." Kate felt the tears coming and took a deep breath to compose herself.

"Knowing what Lane was going through when I first met her makes me keenly aware of the damage I may have done to her ability to trust. She let me in, and I betrayed her." She stifled a sob. "That evening, I started to tell Lane of my intentions, that I want her to be a part of my life. I've probably ruined my chance at that. I know that I can never express to you how very sorry I am, but I want to try. I will keep trying to tell Lane too until she tells me to go away or gives me the chance to make it up to her. I know that you haven't been coming to the potlucks because you don't want to see me. You and Aunt Connie have been friends for a long time and it's killing me that I have caused this tension in your relationship." Kate had been rambling and stopped to take a breath.

"My dear girl, you have an awful lot of guilt on your shoulders." Ellie patted Kate's hand. "Let's take some of that away. First of all, the gala was a huge success, as always. Apart from a few busybodies, no one else knew what had happened. I have not been to the last two potlucks because I have had conflicting engagements not because I did not want to see you. You have not ruined anything between your aunt and me. She and I have been through a lot worse than this little incident, and I'm sure we have more ups and downs to weather in our days left here on this earth." Ellie shook her head.

"But now, about Lane. My granddaughter is very special to me, and as you can imagine, when she hurts, I hurt as well. It was very difficult to see how she was taken advantage of in that last relationship even though some of it was her own fault. She allowed things to happen because she didn't stand up for herself. She knows better. So, when I saw her becoming friends with you, I reminded her that if she wanted to take your relationship in a certain direction, she would be wise to make sure she was very clear about what it was she wanted. From what I understand, Lane did tell you she wanted to see you when she came out to the island, but she didn't give you a clear indication that she wanted it to be exclusive or that she suspected from the beginning that there might have been something going on with you and this other woman."

Kate was taken back by that comment and how much Ellie knew. *Why didn't Lane tell me she thought something was going on between Faith and me?* "Yes, that's basically how it was."

"Well, then, you didn't really do anything wrong dear. Did you?"

"No. Wait. What?" Kate couldn't believe what she was hearing.

"Were you still seeing this woman when you spoke to Lane of your intentions the night of the gala?"

"Technically, no. I had been avoiding her for weeks, but I hadn't told her that I didn't want to see her anymore."

"But if nothing had happened that night, and you and Lane had talked and decided on things, you would have gone to the other woman and broken it off?"

"Yes. I would have done that."

"Then, again, you didn't do anything wrong. It was all in the timing, for both you and Lane."

"Doctor Bellows, I think you're making this a little simpler than it is." Kate sighed and shook her head.

"Please dear, call me Ellie. Just give Lane some time to figure things out. I'm sure once all is revealed, things will work out exactly the way they are supposed to." Ellie gave Kate a comforting smile before getting up to hug her. "Now, I hate to rush you off, but I have guests coming for dinner."

Kate was still a little in shock as she and Ellie walked to the front door. Ellie gave Kate another quick hug and before Kate knew it, she was on the other side of the closed door. *What the hell just happened?* Kate was still trying to absorb it as she drove out of the driveway. Once on the main road and back in control of her faculties, Kate pulled to the side and called Faith. After the good luck she had at Ellie's, Kate figured she was on a roll and didn't want to waste any time tackling the next fear on her list. Faith picked up on the third ring.

"Hello, Kate."

Ah. Caller ID. Of course. Kate was half surprised Faith answered. "I was wondering if we could talk. Can you meet me somewhere?"

"Where are you now?"

"On the island."

"I'm in Sag Harbor. Come and meet me at Cogan's. I'll be at a table."

"I'll be there as soon as I can."

The ferry was so slow Kate was certain she could have swum across the channel faster. When she arrived in Sag Harbor, she drove to Cogan's and parked. She stood next to her car taking deep breaths to calm herself, but it wasn't working. She decided she was as calm as she was going to get and went inside. She spotted Faith at a back table and felt a pang of excitement. *Stop it, Kate. This can't happen. This is not why you're here.*

Faith glanced up from her glass of wine.

"Hey, Faith." Kate started to smile but realized that may not be the best approach.

Faith just stared.

"May I sit down?"

"I wouldn't have agreed to meet you if I didn't anticipate talking to you."

The server approached the table. "May I get you something?" she asked Kate.

"I'll have what she's having."

"Do me a favor?" Faith smiled at the woman and held up her glass of wine. "Just bring a bottle."

Kate waited until the server left before speaking. "Thank you for seeing me. I have some explaining to do."

"Yes, I believe you do."

"First and foremost, please believe that it was never my intention to hurt you. I thought that if one of us found that our relationship wasn't working, we'd tell each other and that we would be adult about it."

Faith didn't say anything.

"The problem was I didn't get a chance to tell you. No, that's not the truth. I wasn't brave enough to tell you. I was selfish and wanted to avoid a confrontation, so I didn't say anything."

Faith took a sip of her wine. "Go on."

"If you had been available from the start, things might not have turned out this way. But when I met Lane, I realized that I want someone who is available and who can be in a relationship with me."

"Rather than sneaking around like with me, you mean?"

"Well, I wouldn't say sneaking around. But I wouldn't have been comfortable going to an event with you if we had to pretend to be friends, especially since I suspect most people would have known the truth anyway."

"I don't think you gave me a chance to change our relationship."

"Come on, Faith. That's not true. That Sunday morning in Southampton and again at dinner that night I told you my feelings for you could develop and what we could have together, but you weren't willing to give up your lifestyle."

Faith took Kate's hand.

"I guess I didn't realize what I could lose. When I become involved in these extramarital relationships, I never allow myself to become too attached because I know I have no intention of them lasting. I have fun for a while and then move on to the next one. That wasn't the case with you. But I know our timing is off and that unless I make changes in my life, you and I can't go on. I just don't know if I'm ready to make those changes now or how long it might take, so I think its best that you and I go our separate ways."

Kate couldn't believe her ears. *Is this real, or is she about to break out in maniacal laughter?* She waited a moment. "Faith, I—"

"Really, Kate. Don't say anything, please. This is quite hard for me as it is, so I think it's best if you just go. Who knows, maybe someday things will be different." Faith's eyes welled up. "Just know that I was falling in love with you, and I won't cause you any trouble. If we see each other around, we can acknowledge each other knowing that what we had was good while it lasted and that we always wish each other nothing but the best."

Kate was crying now too. She got up and gently kissed Faith's cheek. "Nothing but the best," she whispered. Then she turned and left without looking back.

Chapter Thirty-two

THE WEEKS FLEW BY and Kate still hadn't heard from Lane despite the regular messages she left. She left another message while she waited for Constance and Patsy to load their baskets of food into the Range Rover for the Friday night potluck.

"No luck, kiddo?" Patsy asked as she settled in the backseat.

"No," Kate said as she started the car.

"You know, dear, Ellie's birthday is next weekend. There's a good chance that Lane will attend the party," Constance said.

Kate turned her attention to her aunt and off the road long enough to veer slightly off the pavement.

"Watch it there, kid. You're going to make me lose my hat," Patsy said.

"Sorry, Pats. Are you serious, Aunt Connie? Why didn't you tell me this earlier? Where's the party going to be? Can I come?"

"I found out just before we left the house. Ellie wasn't going to do anything for her birthday, but I convinced her otherwise. When you get to a certain age, its best to celebrate your birthday since you never know if it's going to be your last."

"Constance!" Patsy shrieked. "Don't say that."

"Oh, all right. We decided that it might be nice to have a birthday party before everyone leaves for the winter."

"Can I come?" Kate asked again. She steered the Range Rover into Ms. Lawrence's driveway.

"I'm sure you will be invited, dear," Constance said as she climbed out of the car.

Kate carried some of the baskets to the house. She wasn't sure she'd be invited.

***

Kate had been distracted since she found out that Lane would likely be at Ellie's party that weekend and by Wednesday she was pacing her office. Time just wasn't going by fast enough. When not being able to concentrate on work became unbearable, Kate locked up the office and went to the Seagull.

Shannon set a beer on the bar before Kate even had a chance to sit down. "What's going on?" Shannon threw a bar towel over her shoulder.

"Just trying to keep myself from going crazy." Kate picked up the beer and took a sip.

"Good luck with that. So, what's got you?"

"A birthday party for Lane's grandmother that Lane may or may not attend."

"Wouldn't she attend her own grandmother's birthday party?" Shannon gave Kate a puzzled look.

"Not if she has to see me."

"Maybe you're not invited."

"Oh, I got myself an invitation and I'll be there." Kate sat up and smiled.

Shannon laughed and, as if on cue, Kate's cell phone rang.

"Hey, Mom. What's up?" Kate answered after checking the caller ID.

"Hello, darling. I wanted to let you know that you're Dad and I are coming out this weekend."

"Really? Wow. That's great, how come?"

"To see you and Constance. Why else?"

"That's cool, but, just so you know, Aunt Connie and I are going to a party Saturday night."

"I know. We're going too."

"Good. I could use the support in case Lane does or doesn't show up." Kate thought for a moment. "Why are you and Dad going? Do you know Ellie that well?"

"Not really, but the timing worked out for us. Besides, we know enough people on the island who will be there, so it should be fine."

"Okay. Great. See you then. Love you."

"Love you too. Bye, darling."

Kate hung up and turned her attention to Natalie who joined her to get the latest news. Shannon finished with her customer and she too returned to hear the details. Kate told them both everything. "And that brings you up to date and to the party on Saturday."

"I can't believe Faith let you off so easy." Natalie shook her head.

"I think she really cared about Kate," Shannon said.

"Well, whatever it was, I'm glad there wasn't any big drama." Kate took a sip of her beer.

"Maybe she's just waiting to catch you off guard and then, when you least expect it, she'll do something."

"Nat, don't say that." Shannon threw a bar towel at her.

"Please, Nat, don't even think it." Kate held up her hands in surrender.

"Fine, then. I'm sure she's already moved on." Natalie's lack of sincerity was not lost on Kate. "What about Lane?"

"I guess I'll go to the party and see if she's there. If she is, I'll try to talk to her."

"I think she would have contacted you already if she wanted anything to do with you," Natalie said.

"Wow, Nat. Can you be more of a downer?" Kate frowned and shook her head.

"Seriously, Natalie." Shannon turned and went to the kitchen.

"You might be right. I may have lost out on her, and if that's the case, I have no one to blame but myself. I'll go and see what happens." Kate finished her beer and placed some money on the bar.

"Be sure to keep me posted," Natalie said.

"Don't worry, Natalie. I'll be sure you hear all the details in a reasonable amount of time." The two laughed and chatted for another few minutes before Kate decided she was ready to go home.

"Good luck, Kate. Really. I hope it all works out."

"Me too, Natalie. Me too."

Chapter Thirty-three

KATE LEFT THE OFFICE early Friday so she could be home when her parents arrived. Later that evening the three of them joined Constance and Patsy at the Rose and Thistle.

"Is everyone looking forward to tomorrow night's festivities?" Patsy asked during dessert. "It should promise to be an interesting evening."

"Why would that be?" Morgan asked.

"Oh, for heaven's sake, Patsy, that's enough." Constance turned to Morgan and softened her tone. "I think, Morgan dear, that Patsy means it will be a fun evening. Isn't that right, Patsy?"

Patsy looked like the cat that ate the canary. "Yes, that's what I meant."

Afraid of being disappointed, Kate hadn't asked about Lane. Finally, she broke down. "Aunt Connie, have you heard anything about Lane attending?"

"No, dear, I'm sorry. I haven't. I don't think Ellie has been able to get an answer from her."

Kate sat back in her chair, her shoulders hunched. "I'm sure she would have been here by now if she was coming."

Kate went to sleep that night asking for a miracle. She did not feel confident that Lane would be at the party.

***

Kate kept herself as busy as possible with her mother and father out and about on the island. At almost six o'clock, Kate and her parents took the short ride to Ellie's from Belle's Beauty. She was tempted to lurk in the front yard and watch for Lane, but her parents dragged her to the door where they were greeted by a server with glasses of champagne. A small crowd had already gathered and Kate scanned the faces.

Morgan was one step ahead of her. "Not yet, dear-heart."

Kate nodded.

As they made their way through the crowd greeting fellow guests, they heard Patsy call out. "There they are. I was just asking when you were going to get here." She hugged each of them.

"Pats, have you seen her?" Kate asked.

"The birthday girl is with your Aunt Connie around here somewhere." Patsy looked around.

"Lane, Pats. Have you seen Lane?" Kate strained her neck to look around and scan the crowd.

"Oh, of course. Lane. No. Sorry, kiddo. I haven't seen her."

Kate's stomach dropped.

"But what I do know," Patsy said as she lifted Kate's chin with a finger, "is that I'm pretty sure this evening will be full of surprises." Before Kate could probe for details, Patsy was off to greet new guests. "Yoo hoo! Hello! Long time no see—"

"Come on." David put one arm around Kate and the other around Morgan. "Let's check out what's going on."

As they worked their way around the room, they spotted Constance and Ellie holding court. They wished Ellie a happy birthday before Constance whisked her off to greet some other guests.

"Wow, there's really quite a crowd gathering," Morgan said. "Let's get something to eat and settle somewhere. I'd like to eat first and then mingle."

David and Kate followed Morgan to the dining room where a large buffet was set up. Kate kept scanning the crowd but to no avail. There was no sign of Lane.

"Is that all you're eating?" David said, looking at Kate's almost empty plate.

"I'm too upset to eat."

"Eat something, dear-heart. If you get too depressed and start drinking heavily, you'll need a good base in your stomach." Morgan laughed.

"Nice one, Mom. Are you trying to get me to cause another scene?"

"Well, you do need to start building a reputation on the island." Morgan patted Kate's back.

"Such good parents I have." Kate laughed as she shook her head in disbelief.

After David and Morgan finished eating and Kate finished pushing her food around her plate, they went back to socializing. Servers distributed flutes of champagne. Patsy stood at the front of the living room and clinked her glass with a fork.

"Attention everyone. Attention," Patsy bellowed. "May we have your attention please?"

"What's going on?" David whispered.

"I don't know. Let's find out." Morgan started inching her way through the crowd with David and Kate close behind. Constance and Ellie stood at the front of the room and Patsy was seated next to them. Constance smiled when she saw them approaching.

Once everyone settled down, Constance spoke to the crowd. "Good evening everyone. We are so glad you could join us on this very special occasion to wish Ellie a very happy birthday."

The guests applauded and yelled, "Happy Birthday."

"Before I begin, I'd like to call two special people to the front of the room. Where are you girls?" The crowd parted as two people made their way toward Constance and Ellie. "I think you all know Ellie's daughter, Patricia, and Ellie's granddaughter, Lane."

Kate gasped when she heard the words come out of Constance's mouth and stood frozen as she watched Lane make her way to the front of the crowd to hug her grandmother.

Once Lane and Patricia finished greeting Ellie, Constance continued with her speech. "Although many of you in our little group have known this for years, many of you do not, so for the benefit of those who do not, allow me to share with you that Ellie and I are a couple."

Gasps filled the room followed by cheers. Kate's jaw dropped. She looked at her mother, but Morgan's expression told her that she, too, had no clue. Patricia and Lane looked stunned as well.

"Quiet down, everyone. She's not done. Okay. That's enough. Quiet, please." Patsy stood and restored order. "Please, Constance, continue."

"This might come as quite a shock to some of you, but if you know anything about the two of us, it is that we are very private people and we feel that one's love life should not be out for public consumption. But life is short, and love is hard to find. When two people find it, they should take hold of it and never let it go." Constance looked at Kate. "It is with that philosophy in mind that tonight I proudly announce our engagement. Ellie and I are going to be married."

The crowd erupted applause and cheers.

Constance continued speaking over the excitement. "I'd like you to know that you have been invited on this special evening because you are such very good friends of ours and we want to share this evening with you. I would especially like to thank my niece, Morgan, her husband, David, and my great niece, Kate, for being here with me tonight. And I know Ellie is grateful to have Patricia and Lane here as well." Constance raised her glass to the crowd and then to Ellie, who responded with her glass. The two clinked glasses and sipped their champagne as they held hands.

Patsy stood up. "Okay, everyone, let's raise our glasses to the happy couple. To Constance and Ellie."

"To Constance and Ellie!" The crowd cheered and then rushed the happy couple.

Kate, Morgan, and David looked at each other in disbelief.

"Uh, did you guys know about this?" Kate asked.

"Not a thing," Morgan said.

"Did your aunt just come out?" David asked, shaking his head. "Because if she did, I'm more scared of her now than ever." He laughed.

"I guess we should get up there and find out." Morgan made her way toward Constance. David and Kate followed and together they stood in the reception line that had formed. Finally, Morgan reached Ellie. She kissed Ellie on the cheek, and then hugged and kissed Constance. Morgan congratulated them and commented that she'd never seen Constance as happy as she was now. David offered his congratulations as well.

When Kate could stand it no longer, she muscled her way up to her aunt and hugged her, and then Ellie. "Aunt Connie, I'm so happy for you. I think I can speak for Mom and Dad when I say you really surprised us with this announcement."

"I was fairly confident that you wouldn't have much interest in my love life." Constance smiled softly. "But, we will have time later to discuss it once the party's over and it's just family."

"Perhaps by then I can begin to wrap my head around it." Kate joked as she stepped back to allow others waiting in the reception line access to the happy couple.

Kate grabbed another glass of champagne and wandered out to the patio. There was a slight chill in the air, a certain sign that fall was approaching. Kate gazed up at the moonless sky and took in all the stars.

"Penny for your thoughts."

Kate turned and faced Lane.

Lane looked up at the stars as she stepped forward and stood next to Kate. "No doubt you were surprised by their announcement."

"I'll say. You could have knocked me over with a feather."

"How have you been?" Lane turned to look at Kate.

"Me? I'm fine, I guess. Busy with work and humbled by my recent relationship experiences." Kate bowed slightly.

"How is your relationship with Faith?" Lane asked.

"There is no relationship with Faith. There never really was. We have talked since the gala, and luckily she hasn't gone on the warpath or tried to destroy me." Kate smiled ever so slightly.

"Yes. I'm sure Constance can be very convincing, especially with Patsy around."

Kate frowned. "What do you mean?"

"Oh, my. I thought you knew." Lane put her hand to her mouth.

"Knew what?"

"My grandmother told me that Constance and Patsy paid Faith a visit."

"Are you kidding me?" If it had been anyone but Lane telling her this, Kate would not have believed it.

"They apparently met her for lunch and stayed only long enough to make sure she understood she was not to cause you any problems."

"Wow. They really are undercover assassins." Kate shook her head but was unable to hide the smile emerging on her lips.

"Undercover assassins?"

"Oh. Sorry. Inside family joke. That sure does explain things. I would have liked to be a fly on the wall at that lunch."

Kate started to say something else but was cut short by Patsy. "Sorry to bust up your visit, kiddo, but your aunt wants you two to come in for some pictures."

Kate sighed but obliged. She hoped that Lane would be willing to continue their conversation later. She didn't want to get her hopes up, but she had to admit she felt a tinge of excitement just to have had the chance to talk to Lane for a few minutes.

After three more hours of celebrating, the last of the guests finally left. The two families and Patsy settled down in the comfortable living room.

"What a night." Patsy kicked off her shoes and took a long sip of her champagne.

"That looks like a great idea, Patsy." Morgan kicked off her shoes too.

The group fell silent. Kate finally spoke up. "All right, I don't know about the rest of you, but I want some answers, Aunt Connie."

"I'm sure you do dear." Constance took Ellie's hand. "Ellie and I have known each other for many years. At some point along the line, we came to discover our mutual interest in each other." Constance looked at Ellie with deep affection. "I have always known how I felt about her, but she had been married and had children. That was what young ladies were brought up to do back in our day. There were no opportunities to explore other options."

Constance gave the group a quick glance but kept her focus on Ellie. "In my case, I had a loving family who supported my pursuit of happiness and encouraged me to be decisive and live the life I wanted. No one ever questioned me. I have heard it said that I am very assertive and self-confident, a claim I cannot completely deny." Constance chuckled. "I suppose everyone thought I could never find a man strong enough to be my husband."

"So, when I was growing up and you were on your trips with different friends, they were your girlfriends?" Kate asked, trying to piece things together.

"Well, not all of them, dear." Constance blushed. "That would have been quite a love life I had, now wouldn't it? Some of them really were just friends."

Kate looked at Patsy and raised a brow.

"Not me, kiddo, I've only dated men. That was enough trouble." Patsy raised both hands as everyone laughed

Constance kissed Ellie's hand. "But, there's only one woman for me."

"You two have been an item since I've been here?" Kate asked, knowing it was a silly question.

"Well, of course we have. We just kept it a little quieter than usual and toned down our overnight visits."

"Wow. Okay, Aunt Connie. Too much information now, my fault for asking. I'm done." Kate covered her ears with her hands.

Everyone laughed and David lifted his glass. "I guess we're all going to be family now. So, if I may, here's to family."

"Here, here!" They raised their glasses in agreement and sipped their champagne.

"What plans have you two made?" Morgan asked.

"That's something I'd like to know," Patricia said.

"Me, too." Lane raised her hand.

"Well, for starters, we were thinking about moving in together here. And then perhaps a spring wedding." Ellie smiled.

Kate bolted upright. "Wait a minute. You can't leave me all alone, Aunt Connie."

"Now, dear, you'll be just fine. You are busy and you don't need me under your feet every second."

Kate felt sick at the thought of being all alone in that big house. "Can we talk about this?"

Constance shook her finger at Kate. "Nothing is happening tonight, dear. We are just down the block. Besides, you'll want to make the house your own."

"Hey," David interrupted. "You've got us! How about we move in with you?"

Kate sighed. "Aunt Connie's right. I'll be fine."

Patsy stood up. "It's getting late. How about we call it a night?"

"Sounds good to me," Morgan agreed.

"Just leave everything where it is," Ellie said. "I have people coming in the morning to clean up."

Before leaving with her parents, Kate asked Lane, "Are you staying for a few days?"

"Until Tuesday."

"Can we talk?" Kate brushed the tips of Lane's fingers with her hand.

"Why don't you call me tomorrow and we'll see what we can work out." Lane smiled.

Kate went home and went to sleep with a hopeful smile on her face.

Chapter Thirty-four

THE NEXT MORNING KATE found Constance having a cup of tea alone in the kitchen. "You're awake early, dear. Is everything all right?"

"I couldn't sleep. Lane agreed to talk to me today, but it's too early to call. I'm anxious about how this is going to turn out. How come you're up so early?" Kate poured some tea and sat across the table from Constance.

"Oh, I've got a lot of thinking to do." Constance took a sip of her tea.

"Is everything all right?"

"Yes, dear. It's just that since we made the announcement last evening, things seem different." Constance shook her head.

"Different in a good way, I hope?"

"Of course, in a good way, dear. When you get to my age, and you're used to things a certain way, change can be hard."

"Aunt Connie, I think that's true at any age." Kate chuckled.

"I suppose you're right, dear. I need to take things slow and get used to it all."

"I don't think you should have to get used to something if you're truly happy about it."

Constance replied without hesitation. "That's not it at all. I'm happy. Really, I am. I just need to get things settled in my mind. Really, dear, there is no need to be so concerned. I am perfectly fine." She smiled and patted Kate's hand.

"If you say so. But please, Aunt Connie, promise me you'll never do anything you don't want to do."

"My dear, I don't think we are in any danger of that." Constance laughed. "Now, tell me, what's the latest with you and Lane?"

"Hopefully, I'll find out today. She seemed okay last night, but that might mean that she's done with me and that she plans on being cordial when we see each other at family functions." Kate pursed her lips and crunched her brow. "By the way, Lane mentioned something about you and Patsy paying Faith a visit."

"Tsk, tsk, Ellie," Constance whispered.

"What was that all about?"

"Well, dear, you know we were concerned that she might make trouble for you. We thought it best to nip things in the bud. A friendly chat seemed the most appropriate course of action."

"A chat? Is that what you're calling it?" Kate laughed out loud. "And what did this chat involve, exactly?"

"It wasn't as if we followed her down an alley with baseball bats. But, if you must know, we attended a charity event for the East End Animal Rescue and it just so happened that Faith was there."

"It just so happened, huh?"

"Well yes, dear. It's true that we hadn't been to an event for that charity in some time, so we decided that we ought to go. You understand, dear. To make an appearance."

"To make an appearance. Mmmmmm hmmmmmm." Kate waved her hand in the air.

"Okay, perhaps we did know that Faith was going to be at the event, but I assure you that Patsy and I would have gone to the event nonetheless."

"Go on," Kate prodded, forgiving her aunt's likely dishonesty.

"We merely took advantage of the pre-auction social hour to have a chat with her."

"What did you say during this chat?" Kate realized she was getting an inaccurate depiction of the truth, but she couldn't deny that she appreciated the concern that prompted her aunt to approach Faith in the first place.

"I merely informed her that you are my niece and that it might be in her best interest not to make any disparaging remarks against you."

"That's it? And just like that she agreed?" Kate knew Faith better than that. Although hard to believe, Kate swore she saw her aunt squirm in her chair.

"Well, we basically told her that with one phone call we could have her blacklisted from every event between Montauk and Manhattan."

"Aunt Connie, you didn't!" Kate couldn't believe her ears.

"It was for your protection, dear. And I would do it again in an instant." Constance was serious.

"I appreciate that, Aunt Connie, but do you really think she would have done anything?"

"That was not a chance we were about to take, dear." Constance pursed her lips and shook her head.

Kate's eyes began to fill with tears. "Thank you, Aunt Connie."

"Now, dear, you must know there isn't anything I wouldn't do for you."

Kate started to cry. "I'm so sorry, Aunt Connie. All this time I thought you were so...so..."

"Oh there, there, dear." Constance patted Kate's hand again. "I know I haven't always been the easiest to get along with, and there were times I didn't go about things the right way with you. Maybe it was because I didn't have children and didn't know how to communicate properly. Regardless, I should have tried a little harder."

Constance slid her chair closer to Kate. "You know, I was always a little jealous of your relationship with your grandmother, and Belle knew it. But she was a wonderful sister, and rather than be angry with me, she encouraged me to come along and join in your activities. I always declined because I didn't want to intrude. Now I wish I had." Constance paused a moment. "Kate, I want you to know that I have always loved you, and would do anything to protect you." Constance patted the tears from Kate's face with a tissue.

Kate smiled through her tears.

"How about you and I make a deal right now?" Constance took Kate's hand. "I think you and I have done pretty well together these last few months, so why don't we make a promise to keep that going? Let's start a new friendship and concentrate on our new and better understanding of each other. Does that sound all right with you?"

Kate squeezed Constance's hand. "I'd like that." Kate reached out to hug Constance, who stood up and pulled Kate to her feet. The two hugged and Kate felt satisfied with the new direction of their lives.

"Now, let's get ourselves together. You have a big day ahead of you with Lane. Why don't you take a shower, and I'll make us some breakfast? By then, it will be an acceptable hour to phone Lane."

Kate headed toward the stairs, cup of tea in hand. With her foot on the bottom step, she smiled and turned back to Constance. "I'm guessing you could've taken care of Faith with one phone call, couldn't you?"

Never breaking her stride or turning to look at Kate, Constance opened the refrigerator. "Absolutely. But then I would have missed the charity event."

Chapter Thirty-five

IT WAS A LOVELY day, and Lane agreed to meet Kate at one of the town beaches. Kate backed the Mercedes into a parking spot and sat for a moment to calm herself. When she got out of the car, she headed toward the beach but then thought better of it. She wanted to be sure she would see Lane when she pulled in. She leaned against the trunk of the Mercedes and stared out at the beach. It was late in the season and there were few people relaxing in the chairs along the sand. A few minutes later, Lane's car pulled into the parking lot. Lane parked next to Kate and gave her a gentle smile before she got out of the car and joined Kate.

"Hi." Kate wanted to hug Lane, but she was afraid to move. "Thanks for coming."

Lane leaned against the car next to Kate and scanned the water line. "We need to talk, Kate."

Kate's stomach dropped. *Oh no, the dreaded 'we need to talk' line.*

Lane turned so that she stood in front of Kate. "I have to apologize to you."

Kate was taken back. "Apologize? You? For what?"

"Overreacting, and then being too immature to admit it."

"Lane, I think you have things backwards here."

"I knew that night at the Seagull that you were seeing Faith, and I was all right with that. I'd just come out of a bad relationship and I was frightened by the thought of starting a new one. I was okay with us seeing each other casually when I came to the island and I was okay knowing you were seeing other people. But once we saw more of each other, things started to change. That night at the gala, the thought that you were still seeing Faith got to me and I didn't want to be made a fool of again." Lane paused for a moment and took a deep breath. "I suppose the real truth isn't that I was afraid you were seeing Faith, but that you might have serious feelings for her."

"I understand. Once bitten, twice shy. But what happened that night at the gala was my fault. I wanted to be with you, but I hadn't broken it off with Faith because I was a chicken shit. I wanted to tell you that night, but I didn't get the chance before everything blew up." Kate's eyes welled up with tears.

"Well, that's why I'm apologizing. I knew you wanted to talk that night. I wonder if you will give me another chance?"

"You're kidding, right? I think it's you who needs to give me another chance to prove I can make you happy."

"So." Lane put her arms around Kate's waist. "Should we try this again?"

"Absolutely," she said before leaning in to kiss her. Kate's anxiety was lifted. She felt a surge of excitement course through her. The two kissed in between giggles for a little longer before either of them spoke.

"Does this mean we're going to be related?" She laughed.

Kate laughed too. "Oh, you and I are going to be so related." Kate pressed herself against Lane and kissed her hard and long before releasing her. Then she took her by the hand and headed toward the beach. Half way to the water, the two sat down in the sand.

"Did you have any clue about your aunt and my grandmother?" Lane asked.

"Not at all. Not about any of it. I wonder how I could have been so clueless."

"Well, you told me that you never really spent too much one-on-one time with your aunt."

"I suppose, but still, no clue whatsoever?" Kate shook her head. "From the look on your face at the party, I'm guessing you didn't know either."

"I knew the two of them went to the City together and spent the night at each other's houses, but I didn't think anything of it. I just thought they were doing things that best friends do."

Thinking back, Kate realized she may have missed some clues as well. "You know, Patsy has made a few off-handed remarks recently, but I just thought that was Patsy being Patsy. Now that I think about it, my aunt had a luncheon the day of the estate transfer and there was an extra place setting at the table. I couldn't figure it out before, but now I think I get it. I bet it was for your grandmother. I imagine there should have been two extra place settings, but you had already left the island. Patsy knew something was up that day, too."

"When was that?"

"The Wednesday after the gala."

Lane thought for a moment. "I think you're right. I bet the plan was for me to be there as well. My grandmother had invited me to lunch during the week, but I couldn't clear my schedule."

"Those two are too much, I bet they planned on making the announcement to us before the party as a way of getting us in the same room together. I could see them plotting that. It was such an emotional day for me, and they probably thought we would get swept up in their happiness and get back together." Kate nodded.

"Regardless," Lane said, "the important thing is that we're together now and all of us are happy."

"I like that." Kate kissed Lane's hand and then stood up, pulling Lane up with her. "Come on. Let's go back to the house and see what's going on."

Kate was not surprised to see Patsy's car in the driveway when she pulled in. As she neared the house, Kate caught a glimpse of Patsy and Constance scrambling to get out of view. *Ah ha, they've been watching and waiting. I shouldn't be surprised.* She got out of her car and waited for Lane. The two headed toward the house hand in hand.

"I think we have an audience," Kate said.

"What do you mean?"

"You didn't see the scrambling bodies on the patio? Patsy and Aunt Connie were practically falling over each other to get out of sight."

When they got to the patio, Kate laughed out loud. It was worse than she had thought. Gathered around the table were Constance, Ellie, Patsy, Morgan, and David.

"Oh, there you are, dear," Constance said, acting surprised to see them. "I see you have Lane with you. Why don't you both come and have a drink?" Constance waved them over to the table. Kate and Lane pulled up chairs and made themselves comfortable.

When Patsy could take it no longer, she burst. "Oh, come on, kids, don't leave us in suspense. It sure looks like you two are back together. Is it as it looks? Are you two back together or not?"

Kate looked at Lane, but she only gave Kate a wide grin. Kate took that as her cue. "Yes, we are."

Applause erupted around the table, and David pulled a bottle of champagne out from its hiding place.

Morgan got up from her seat and kissed them both. "We couldn't be happier for you. What are your plans?"

"Mom, really. We just got back together thirty minutes ago. We haven't gotten that far." Kate laughed.

"I think Lane should move her practice out here, and then they both can work from home," Ellie said.

"That's perfect," Patsy said. "Don't you agree, Lane?"

"We haven't discussed any of that yet," Lane said, her voice cracking a little. Questions started coming at full speed from all directions. Sensing Lane's increasing discomfort, Kate whistled to get everyone's attention.

"Hold on a minute. We're going to need some time to figure this all out, okay? I suggest in the meantime we keep the champagne flowing and talk about anything else except what Lane and I plan to do with the rest of our lives."

Accepting the chastisement and redirection, they sat in silence until David poured the champagne and they each had a glass in hand. Kate offered a toast. "To my family and this island. Nothing makes me happier."

Chapter Thirty-six

A LIGHT SNOW FELL as Kate put wood on the fire. Christmas was only a few days away and her parents would be arriving at any moment. Before taking one last walk through the house, Kate stopped to look at the Christmas tree. It was beautiful and covered in decorations, some old, some new, and it warmed Kate's heart. Kate ended her walk in the guest bedroom. She spotted nothing out of place and was satisfied the house was ready for her guests. Her grandmother's bedroom now belonged to her and Lane. They had painted the room light green and bought some new furnishings, but they also kept some pieces that belonged to Belle.

Lane moved in at the beginning of December. Kate kept her apartment in Manhattan for them and Lane gave up her rental. It had taken her a few months to work out an arrangement with her practice in the City. She would go to the City one week of each month to see patients and Kate would join her as much as her busy practice on the island allowed. Lane planned to start her own practice on the island as well.

"Hey," Kate called out. "Where are you?"

Lane came out of the bathroom. "I was just putting some more things away."

"Okay, but you have to stop now. My parents should be here any minute. Besides, everything looks great."

"Did you hear from Aunt Connie?"

"Yes. She and your grandmother were getting their things together. They'll pick up Patsy and be here shortly."

Constance and Ellie decided that since neither of them wanted to give up their homes, they would split their time between houses. They stayed a week or so with Kate and Lane and then went to Ellie's for a week or so. The arrangement felt a little strange at first, but it was working out well.

"I can't wait for everyone to get here for our first Christmas." Lane couldn't hide her excitement as she hugged Kate.

"I can't wait for my parents to see the house."

Kate and Lane had repainted some rooms and updated some of the furniture here and there but little else. At first, Kate held off on making many changes to the house, fearing she would feel the loss of her grandmother's presence. But deep down, Kate knew that her grandmother would always be near her heart no matter what the color schemes in the house or the furniture that filled it. *In time. In time. Lane and I have the rest of our lives for redecorating.*

"I'm excited for them to see the house too," Lane said.

"I know what you really want my mother to see." Kate took Lane's hand and guided her to the foot of their bed.

"I can't deny it. It was my salvation, and in the end, it helped me find my way to you." Lane gazed at the wall above the bed where Sunlight in the Shadows hung.

"You'll never be lost again. Never again."

The End

About Gail Newman

Gail is a native of Long Island, New York, currently living and working near Virginia Beach. Discovering a long-forgotten manuscript, Gail was excited with the prospect of trying her hand at writing again. Her mind opened to new ideas which culminated in her writing Sunlight in the Shadows.

Excited with new thoughts and ideas, Gail plans to continue writing and sharing her stories.

Gail and wife Elise split their time between Virginia and their second home on Shelter Island which they love to fill with friends and family.

Note to Readers:

Thank you for reading a book from Desert Palm Press. We have made every effort to edit this book. However, typos do slip in. If you find an error in the text, please email lee@desertpalmpress.com so the issue can be corrected.

We appreciate you as a reader and want to ensure you enjoy the reading process. We would like you to consider posting a review on your preferred media sites such as Amazon, Smashwords, Bella Books, Goodreads, Tumblr, Twitter, Facebook, and/or your blog or website.

For more information on upcoming releases, author interviews, contest, giveaways and more, please sign up for our newsletter and visit us as at Desert Palm Press: www.desertpalmpress.com and "Like" us on Facebook: Desert Palm Press.

Bright Blessings

www.ingramcontent.com/pod-product-compliance
Lightning Source LLC
Chambersburg PA
CBHW071201260626
47162CB00003B/1126